"A stunning return to his world of *Central Station*, twinning the fates of humans and robots alike at a futuristic city on the edge of the Red Sea."
—*Green Man Review*

"This is Tidhar at his best: the crazily proliferating imagination, the textures, the ideas, the dazzling storytelling. A brilliant portrait of community and its possibilities."
—Adam Roberts, author of *Purgatory Mount*

"This was superb and I'm in awe of Tidhar's vision. He's conjured up a futuristic city that feels simultaneously ultramodern and also run down. The rich histories of the region and its cultures are seamlessly interwoven into the fabric of this fully realized world. Tidhar writes beautifully."
—*The Speculative Shelf*

"A deliciously inventive wild ride through a future Middle East full of unexpected wonders: dutiful jackals, traumatized robots, terrifying terrorartists, caravans of elephants and great slinkying robotic khans, preserves for wild mechas and monasteries that are also singularities. But more than that, the world of *Neom* is deeply, richly lived in: the past and the present and the future are not just unevenly distributed, they are marbled together—tiny slithering tadpole robots adapted to the fused-glass desert around an ancient crash site, okra and tomatoes frying in a pan, rogue sandworms and grandmothers doing Tai Chi in an urban park, the Oort cloud and milkshakes, Martian soap opera Bedouin actors, a Bazaar of Rare and Exotic Machines equally excited by Atari Pac-Man cartridges and

city-obliterating superweapons. It is this eye for detail, this deft touch intermingling now and someday, that makes *Neom*'s future so vividly real: not just human or gritty or lived-in, but full to bursting with the variety and complexity that characterize life. It is a world anchored by its characters: the bright ambition and yearning of the orphan Saleh, the sensible pragmatism and inexhaustible humanity of the capable housecleaner/flower vendor/receptionist/Tamagotchi shelter volunteer Miriam de la Cruz . . . and the robot, who is obsolete and dangerous, full of grief and mystery and philosophy, and whose obstinate mission beckons us ever forward through *Neom*'s pages. . . ."
—Benjamin Rosenbaum, author of *The Unraveling*

"Yet again, Lavie Tidhar's future world of *Neom* is exciting and distinctive, his characters complex and fascinating, and his themes powerful and thought-provoking. [Tidhar] is the best sort of science fiction."
—Kij Johnson, author of *The River Bank*

"Vivid and techno-mythological, *Neom* infects you with something special that transcends all the incidents and terrors—a shimmering current of guarded optimism."
—David Brin, author of *Existence*, *Earth* and *The Postman*

"*Neom* is a treasure, and Tidhar says that there are so many more stories from this complicated world. Every new one is a compelling chapter in this future history that reflects so much about who we are and the basic things we yearn for."
—*SciFi Mind*

"Always expect the unexpected with Lavie Tidhar, and this welcome return to the sprawling space-operatic world of *Central*

Station delivers oodles of poetry, action, memorable characters, wonderfully bizarre landscapes and wild imagination. No two books by Tidhar are ever the same, but each is a revelation."
—Maxim Jakubowski, author of *The Piper's Dance*

PRAISE FOR *CENTRAL STATION*

John W. Campbell Award Winner
Neukom Literary Arts Award Winner
Arthur C. Clarke Award Finalist
NPR Best Books
Barnes and Noble Best Science Fiction and Fantasy
***Locus* Recommended Reading List**

"Beautiful, original, a shimmering tapestry of connections and images."
—Alastair Reynolds, author of the Revelation Space series

"A dazzling tale of complicated politics and even more complicated souls. Beautiful."
—Ken Liu, author of *The Paper Menagerie* and *The Grace of Kings*

★ "Readers of all persuasions will be entranced."
—*Publishers Weekly*, starred review

★ "A fascinating future glimpsed through the lens of a tight-knit community."
—*Library Journal*, starred review

"If Nalo Hopkinson and William Gibson held a séance to channel the spirit of Ray Bradbury, they might be inspired to

produce a work as grimy, as gorgeous, and as downright sensual as *Central Station*."
—Peter Watts, author of *Blindsight* and *The Freeze-Frame Revolution*

"It is just this side of a masterpiece—short, restrained, lush—and the truest joy of it is in the way Tidhar scatters brilliant ideas like pennies on the sidewalk."
—*NPR Books*

"A mosaic of mind-blowing ideas and a dazzling look at a richly-imagined, textured future."
—Aliette de Bodard, author of *The House of Shattered Wings*

"Tidhar weaves strands of faith and science fiction into a breath-taking and lush family history of the far future."
—Max Gladstone, author of *Three Parts Dead*

Selected Books by Lavie Tidhar

Novels
The Bookman (2010)
Osama (2011)
The Violent Century (2013)
A Man Lies Dreaming (2014)
Central Station (2016)
Candy (2018)
Unholy Land (2018)
Adler (2020, graphic novel series with Paul McCaffery)
By Force Alone (2020)
The Escapement (2021)
The Hood (2021)
Maror (2022)

Anthology Series
The Apex Book of World SF, Volumes 1–3 (2009–14)

Lavie Tidhar
Neom

TO NEO-NEANDERTHAL
SANCTUARY

Harrat al Harrah
Mecha Zone

JORDANIAN
PROBABILITY
ZONE

Al-Tubaiq Hazardous Zone
– Beware of Worm Activity

Halat Ammar

Al Khanafah Wild
Machine Sanctuary

THE KINGDOM

Neom

TO MECCA

LAVIE TIDHAR
NEOM

TACHYON   SAN FRANCISCO

Interior and cover design by Elizabeth Story
Interior author photo by Kevin Nixon; copyright © 2013 by Future Publishing
Cover author photo by Krol and Sebastian © 2020

Tachyon Publications LLC
1459 18th Street #139
San Francisco, CA 94107
415.285.5615
www.tachyonpublications.com
tachyon@tachyonpublications.com

Series Editor: Jacob Weisman
Editor: Jill Roberts

Print ISBN: 978-1-61696-382-8
Digital ISBN: 978-1-61696-383-5

Printed in the United States by Versa Press, Inc.

First Edition: 2022
9 8 7 6 5 4 3 2 1

*T*HE CITY OF NEOM *in these pages is* old.

The city of Neom today *remains mostly the dream of a Saudi prince, a futuristic wonderland backed by a marketing video.*

You can go visit it, though. Neom Bay Airport (IATA: NUM, ICAO: OENN) is real and there's even a weekly flight from Riyadh.

There's not much else there right now, but then again, who knows? In time there might be flowers and, if so, a robot might come to the souq one day to buy a rose.

1.
THE CITY

BEYOND CENTRAL STATION, that vast spaceport that links Earth with the teeming worlds of the solar system, there is a city. The city lies past the Gulf of Aqaba and the Straits of Tiran, in the old Saudi desert province that was once called Tabuk. The founders of the city called it Neom.

In sandstorm season the hot air is cooled down by gusts of wind blown into the wide boulevards of the city. The solar fields and wind farms that stretch from beyond the city proper deep into the inland desert capture all the energy Al Imtidad needs, feeding it back to serve all the city's needs.

On the shores of the Red Sea the sunbathers gather. The bars are open late. The kuffar sit smoking sheesha as children run laughing on the beach. Suntanned youths kite-surf in the wind. It is said it's always spring in Neo-Mostaqbal, in Neom. It is said the future always belongs to the young.

Mariam de la Cruz, who came trudging down Al Mansoura Avenue, was no longer so young, though she did not consider herself in the least bit old. It was more of that in-between time, when life finds a way to remind you of both what you'd lost and what lay still ahead.

Of course she was perfectly fine. But she was minutely aware of the ticking clock of senescence on the cellular level. Or in other words, ageing. Which was a problem in a city like Neom, which had been built and then sold—floated on the stock exchanges of Nairobi Prime and Gaza-Under-Sea and Old Beijing—on the premise that *anything* can be fixed, made good, made better, that things do not have to remain the way they'd been.

In Neom, everything was meant to be beautiful, ever since the young prince Mohammad of the Al Saud dynasty first dreamed up the idea of building a city of the future in the desert of the Arabian Peninsula and along the Red Sea. Now it was a mammoth metropolitan area.

Al Imtidad, the locals called it. The urban sprawl.

Mariam had grown up there, had never known another place. Her mother came to Neom from the Philippines in search of work, had met Mariam's father, a truck driver from Cairo who knew the desert roads from Luxor to Riyadh, from Alexandria to Mecca.

He was dead now, her father, had died in a collision on the border of Oman, delivering Chinese goods to the markets of Nizwa. She still missed him.

Her mother had lived on, remarried once, was now in a care facility on the edge of town, in the Nineveh Quarter. Much of what Mariam made went on paying the fees. It was a good place, her mother was well cared for. In the old days families would live together, would look after each other. But now there was only Mariam.

Now she walked, slowly in the heat, cars zooming past her in all directions. Latest model Bohrs, a Faraday roadster, a Gauss II black cab. No one ever named cars after poets, she thought. Her own taste in poetry ran to the neo-classical: Ng Yi-Sheng, Lior Tirosh. They weren't the most famous, they just . . . were.

The cars swarmed around her, ferrying people every which way. They resembled the movement of fish flocks, the way they flowed independently yet in unison. It was illegal to drive a car in Al Imtidad. They were all run by an inference engine. It was usually the way of things, Mariam had found. People didn't trust other people for things like driving them, or for making investment decisions, or for medical care.

Unless, of course, it was a matter of *status*.

Al Mansoura Avenue, on the outskirts of midtown, was a pleasant road with many equally spaced palm trees providing shade along the pavements on either side. The buildings were only a few stories tall, shops on the ground floor and nice spacious apartments above. Dog-walkers walked other people's dogs and nannies pushed other people's babies along the pavements. Cafés were open, blasting out cool air, and the patrons who sat sipping cappuccinos were busy interacting with each other in a meaningful manner, signalling to any passerby that they were not merely relaxing but engaging in important face-to-face connectivity.

The shuttle plane to Central Station flew low overhead. Mariam passed the cafés, the shops selling cultivated pearls and imported perfumes, anti-drone privacy kits, an artisanal bakery wafting out the smell of fresh sourdough loaves and sticky baklawah. A florist stall sold bouquets of fat red roses. The people who lived on Al Mansoura were the upwardly-mobile, and they lived on hope. Hope was a powerful drug.

Another shop, this one renting out luxury watches. She never understood that desire to wear these overpriced, tiny mechanical machines that measured time. Her own watch was a plastic knock-off from the roadside markets in Nineveh, mass-produced in Yiwu, shipped across the world on the Silk Road that China built. The sort of junk her father would have ferried in his truck. But people wore watches to tell the world they were rich, successful, that they were going places. That they took time *seriously*.

Mariam did too. She was paid by the hour. Now she made her way to the address and punched in the code and rode up in the elevator to the Smirnov-Li apartment. It was a nice spacious apartment, with floor-to-ceiling windows overlooking the city and the sea far in the distance. The sort of place that was always rented because it was too expensive to own.

Hardly anyone owned their own place on Al Imtidad. Everything in Neom was rented—living spaces, luxury watches, people.

Smirnov and Li weren't in. Mariam filled a bucket with warm soapy water in their gleaming bathroom. They were a nice, handsome couple, men in their early thirties, their wedding photos hanging in the living room from some beachside ceremony in Fiji or Bali, anyway one of those places people always went to get married in. While Neom's land belonged still to the Saudis, the Committee for the Promotion of Virtue and the Prevention of Vice—the Mutaween—had no power beyond the border, and Mutaween agents had no power of enforcement within the sprawl. Neom's freedom had been part and parcel of the pitch package long before it ever had stocks for sale, when it was still just a corporate promo on a video-sharing site, some wealthy prince's unlikely, faintly ridiculous dream.

As Mariam cleaned the windows she stared out at the city. She liked having the apartment to herself, imagined herself living there, in all that minimalist simplicity. Sometimes Smirnov or Li would be there, but mostly they left her alone to do her job. It was a Neom thing. She knew from the last time she'd seen them that they had been talking about having children, which caused an argument since Smirnov (she never learned their first names, which was another Neom thing) was pushing and Li was resisting, worrying about the costs of an exowomb and arguing over the baby's eye colour.

She cleaned and vacuumed, fed the fish, dusted the shelves, took out the trash and dumped it into the automatic recycling chute.

If people were any poorer they just used some general-purpose household robot. If they were much poorer, they cleaned by themselves. If they were much richer, they had live-in staff. Li and Smirnov were at just the right income level to employ a human cleaner on a part-time basis. Just enough to drop casually in conversation, "Oh, yes, we just had the cleaner in yesterday," and so on. "Lives down in

Nineveh, the poor thing." They were nice people and they paid her well enough, and on time, which meant something. They always told her she could have whatever was in the fridge but, whenever she opened the gleaming chrome door, all she found inside were probiotic yoghurts. People in Neom took care of their gut bacteria the way people in other places looked after their children. Which is to say, personally.

When she left the apartment that afternoon she was hot and she was hungry, and she grabbed a falafel at a roadside stall. Oil ran down her chin and she wiped it with a paper napkin, not caring for the moment about the heat or anything else. Everybody loved falafel. A street was not a street if it didn't have at least one vendor on it.

She passed a branch of the old Banque Nationale de Djibouti, looking for her friend, Hameed. He could usually be found on the corner there.

Then she saw him, sitting as usual with his back to the wall of the bank. Looking up at the sun.

But something was wrong. Something about his posture, his stillness. She took a step forward and another. Then the wrongness intensified and she began to run.

When she reached him, for just a moment, she couldn't take it in. His face, usually so animated, was slack, the smooth skin scorched and torn, the head itself pummelled senselessly until it hung crooked from his neck. His left eye had been gouged from its socket and hung loose over his face. One of his arms was broken and his knees had been smashed, the whole motionless body crudely destroyed and left for dead.

"My God," Mariam said. "My God."

Her fingers stroked his cheek, tracing the soft flesh rubber. The biometric skin had been torn in chunks from the face, revealing the crude mechanical skull and brain behind it. It too had been bashed and broken, and the automaton sat lifeless against the wall.

"Hameed?" Mariam said. "Hameed?"

But there was no response. The one remaining eye stared into nothing. Mariam was shaken, for this was a kind of violence she had seldom experienced, and Hameed was her friend.

He had been a general purpose caregiver-automaton, the sort they used to have installed in old people's homes. He was old, had been made obsolete years before. Usually they'd dump the mannequins afterwards into recycling but Hameed escaped that fate and lived out on the street. He was always very chatty and he smiled a lot and people seemed to like him.

She wiped her eyes. Stood up, looked at the damage. It must have been kids, teenagers who did this. With crowbars or anything crude, some sort of bat. Mariam shook with anger. She called the shurta.

Other passersby went round, ignoring the sight of the broken automaton. On a balcony on the other side of the road, two women were having tea. A fruit-juice seller went past with his cart. A group of Djibouti bankers went past in faded suits.

Djibouti, situated on the Horn of Africa and the Gate of Tears, was the central hub of underwater cables linking Asia, Africa and Europe. They had gradually gained in political and economic importance as the digital overlaid the physical.

But they paid no attention to Hameed, either.

It wasn't long before a shurta cruiser pulled up, and an officer stepped out. The car was a sporty Marconi, striped green and white, with a curved sword on the side, and the officer was slightly less sporty, but with neatly trimmed black hair and polished shoes and an easy smile.

"Hey, Mariam," he said.

"Nasir," she said, relieved. She had known him since kindergarten, his mother had been friends with Mariam's. "I didn't know you worked midtown."

"I'm a sergeant now," he said, smiling a little self-consciously. "What seems to be the problem, Mariam?"

"It's Hameed," she said. "He's been murdered."

Nasir dropped the smile and approached the prone body of the automaton. He knelt down to look at the damage.

"I'm sorry," he said.

"You knew him?"

"Everyone knew Hameed. He was practically a fixture of the neighbourhood."

"So? Can you do something? Can you catch whoever did this?"

Nasir straightened. Looked at her closely.

"Would you like some tea?" he said. "There is a place around the corner from here."

"Can you catch them!" she said.

"Mariam, it's not a person," Nasir said. "It's just a chatbot with a face. It was designed to be appealing to people, but there was no consciousness, nothing but a set of pre-scripted responses in a neural network. It's not like one of the *real* robots, the old humanoid ones they made for the old wars."

"But you can't—!" she said. "You can't just not—"

"I could get them for property damage," he said, "only Hameed wasn't anyone's property, he was, well, discarded. I suppose someone would have to clean it up, so maybe you could get them on littering. Yes—" He brightened. "Littering is a serious crime. We're always on the lookout for—"

But she was no longer listening to him. She nodded, politely, when he spoke, and when he offered her tea again she shook her head, No, thank you, and Yes, I'm quite all right, and then he called it in to the street maintenance crew to come and clean up, and then he was gone again.

But before he'd left he said, "Look, it was really nice running into you again." He shifted from foot to foot.

"Would you like to, I don't know, go out for dinner one night? Catch up on old times, you know . . ." He trailed off.

"Sure," she said. "Sure. I'd like that."

"All right, then." And he smiled that beaming smile again. "Then I guess I'll see you."

"I'll see you, Nasir."

Then he was gone, and she was left alone with the robot.

Mariam took the bus. Like the other vehicles it was fully automated and air-conditioned, and it took her away from midtown and to the edges. As she approached Nineveh Quarter the streets became a little dirtier (but not too dirty) and the wind carried more sand. When she stepped out of the bus the sun was setting and over the desert she could hear the rumble of thunder. She slipped on her sunglasses and walked the rest of the way, dogs barking, children running barefoot, market stalls spilling out their wares. This was where the very many human workers of the city lived: the cooks and cleaners and the waiting staff, the manicurists and the hair stylists, housekeepers, nurses and security guards, the ushers and attendants.

People like her. People who thought even an old robot might be a friend, not just a thing to throw away when you were done with it. She went to visit her mother at the home. Her mother looked good today, more vibrant, talking animatedly when Mariam came in.

"Your father will be back tonight," her mother said. "And we'll go out for dinner, and then to that halo-halo place you like. Wouldn't that be nice?'

"Yes, Mama. It will be very nice," Mariam said. Her father was long dead, and the halo-halo place closed down years earlier. She said, "I saw Hameed today."

"The robot? You always liked him," her mother said. "Ever since you were a little girl. They're good with kids."

Her mother had worked in just such a home as she'd ended up in. That was where Mariam had met Hameed. Her mother could remember the past with startling clarity. It was the present that forever evaded her grasp.

"Yes," Mariam said. "Are you well, Mama?"

Her mother's hand rested on hers. Mariam looked at her mother's hand and marvelled at its spots and wrinkles, remembering again being a child, her mother's strong hands, how gently she'd wash her in the bath. The hands unlined then, and still unmarked by years and the ravages of time.

"I'm well, Mariam. You worry too much." Her mother sat back and sighed. "Your father will be back soon . . . then we'll go out for dinner. We can stop at that halo-halo place you like so much. What do you think, love?"

"I'd like that, Mama," Mariam said.

Mariam took her shopping through the thronged streets to her apartment block. It had started to rain and the mud over-flowed through the broken slab stones of the street. Kids rode around on electric scooters and shopkeepers put out hurricane lamps to hang from their awnings, as the power to this part of the city was often cut unexpectedly if it were needed elsewhere. When she got to her building at last the elevator wasn't working again. She climbed the stairs, at last reaching the apartment. She unlocked the door. In the small kitchen, she chopped garlic, set a pot of okra in tomato sauce to cook. She went to the balcony, lit a rare, illicit tobacco cigarette. One of her neighbours sold them and, on a night like this, no one was going to report her.

She stood on the balcony, looking out to the desert beyond the city. Lightning flashed out in the direction of Mecca, and the wind howled up here, driving with it rain-sodden sand.

She thought about the broken automaton, and whether Li and Smirnov would decide to have that baby and, if so, what colour eyes it'd have. She thought about the little money she'd been saving up, each month, after all the bills and the expenses on her mother. She thought about Nasir, and whether she would call him back.

It would be nice, she thought, to have someone to bring her flowers.

2.
THE CARAVAN

AROUND THE SAME TIME and some three hundred miles away as the quail flies, a boy was watching the approach of a Green Caravanserai from the top of an abandoned tower situated on the Ghost Coast of the Sinai Desert.

The boy's name was Saleh.

He watched the caravaners' approach.

The great khans slinkied across the sand, building and rebuilding themselves as they moved.

Between them came goats and slithering robots. Solar kites soared high above on the winds. Distant robed figures walked with the herds and children ran between the great khans.

Behind them all came the elephants.

The outlines of empty swimming pools dotted the landscape between Saleh and the caravaners. Bavarian castles jostled against Egyptian pyramids. A vintage American diner sat next to an abandoned Alhambra still maintained by rusty robots.

The Ghost Coast ran all the way from the ancient border with what was now the entwined dual polity of the Digitally Federated Judea Palestina Union to Sharm El-Sheikh near the tip of the peninsula.

Beyond it lay the Sinai, eternal and hostile to humans as it had always been.

Saleh gathered his courage. He slid down stairwells and in and out of windows. For just a moment he thought he saw the silhouette of a woman standing beside one of the empty swimming pools. She turned and looked at him and then she vanished, if she was there at all.

He put the apparition out of his mind and headed to the Green Caravanserai.

It was not *protocol* to go alone. The Abu-Ala foraged the Ghost Coast for old machines and they had long ago made arrangements with the caravaners, so Saleh would be going against both tribe wishes and simple decorum.

But he had nothing lose. He had nothing but despair.

He crossed the road and came to the perimeter of the Caravanserai and stopped.

A strange caravaner boy with goggles slid down from the top of a khan tower and came to meet him. He stopped just behind the invisible line.

The two boys stared at each other.

Saleh wasn't going to let them intimidate him. Even though he *was* intimidated.

Two tiny crawling robots came over the line and examined him with feelers extended. Saleh felt hidden weapons trained on him.

The other boy said, "Try not to move."

Saleh stood very still. He took a deep breath. He said, "My name is Saleh Mohammed Ishak Abu-Ala Al-Tirabin."

At this the other boy looked more interested. "You are an Abu-Ala?"

"Yes."

"You are not the designated contact," the boy said.

"No."

"So why are you here?"

Saleh was sweating, though the air was chilly. He said, "I have something."

"So?"

"Something to trade."

The boy looked interested again. "Is it valuable?" he said.

"I think so."

The boy seemed to consider. "Still," he said. "We deal with the tribe, not with individual scavengers. It makes everything easier. Safe."

Saleh said, "There is only me."

"Excuse me?"

Saleh swallowed.

"There is only me," he said quietly.

And then he started to cry.

The other boy's name was Elias. Saleh sat miserably on a mat while Elias brewed sage tea.

Saleh accepted the tea gratefully.

Elias brought out pistachios and hard biscuits. He set them on a plate and sat cross-legged opposite Saleh.

"What happened to them?" he said. He spoke gently.

Saleh shrugged.

"We were excavating in Dahab," he said. "It used to be a robotnik nest during the second, no, maybe the third war. You must have seen the satellite pictures of Dahab, right? It had a terrorartist attack in the fourth war and the whole place is suspended in a sort of still-ongoing explosion, but if you wear a null suit you can navigate through the temporality maze—anyway. We were digging. Dahab's full of valuable old stuff, it's just hard to get. Then, something . . . broke loose." He blinked. "I don't know what. A ghost."

"A *ghost*?" Elias said.

Saleh shrugged again, helplessly. "One of the old Israeli robotniks, I think. It was still alive somehow, inside the explosion. Most power sources don't work inside the terrorartist installation so we bring in portable fusion generators when we go in. I think my father brushed too close to the old robotnik and somehow it drew power from the generator and, and it came alive. They were cyborgs, with biological brains but mostly machine otherwise. I don't even know if it was *alive* in any real sense, only responding to what it saw as battle. So it came loose and it killed my father and the rest of. . . . It killed everyone.'

"I am sorry," Elias said.

Saleh closed his eyes. The tea cup felt warm between his hands.

"Everyone else was away," he said quietly. He had to get the words out. Had to tell Elias what happened. In a way it was a relief.

"Most of the tribe's down in Sharm or St. Catherine's. But I got it, you see." He opened his eyes and stared at the other boy, this Elias, with his strange goggles and short cropped hair and curious, interested gaze.

"You got it? What?" the boy said.

"The thing we were looking for." Excitement quickened in him then. "My grandfather Ishak and my father, Mohammed, they kept looking. Even though it was dangerous. Even though it was hard. Every year the terrorartist bubble moves outwards just a little. It is still alive, the explosion still happening. You know much about terrorart?"

"A little. Rohini started it, didn't she? The Jakarta Event."

"Time-dilation bombs," Saleh said. "Yes, Rohini. There were others. 'Mad' Rucker who seeded the Boppers on Titan. Sandoval, who made the installation called *Earthrise* out of stolen minds on the moon. There were never many. And they were mass murderers, every one. But the art, I know people are still interested in it."

"There are collectors," Elias said. "Museums, too. What did you find?"

"This," Saleh said, simply. He opened his bag and took out a small metal canister. It felt so light. "It's the time-dilation bomb."

Silent alarms must have gone off somewhere, because a

moment later he had caravaners and drones both surround him. He never even heard them coming.

Elias let out a slow exhalation of breath. "And how did we miss that?" he said.

"It's empty," Saleh said. "The explosion, Dahab, everything? It's still going on. My father, my uncle, they're still inside it. An endless death, still happening. The robotnik pulled them into the field. Only I got out."

He didn't dare move. The weapons were on him.

Elias said, "May I see it?"

"Of course."

Saleh gave it to the other boy.

He could see numbers dance behind Elias's goggles. Elias nodded and the weapons around Saleh relaxed, if only a little.

Elias said, "It's genuine. That's a real find."

"I told you," Saleh said, defiant.

"You speak for your tribe?" Elias said.

"I speak for myself."

"And the Abu-Ala? Where do the rest of your people stand on this?" Elias said.

Saleh shook his head. Carefully. "This is mine," he said. "It is all that is left. The others will appoint a new speaker in time."

"What do you want for this?"

"I want enough," Saleh said. He was desperate. "It's priceless, an original terrorartist artefact."

"That is it." Elias turned it over in his hands. Saleh knew it was lighter than it looked.

Elias said, "What do you need the money *for*?"

Saleh said, "There is nothing for me here. I want to go away. Far away. I thought. . . ." He stared into a space only he could see. "There's a place called Central Station. It's just the other side of the sea, and then beyond the desert. They say you can find anything there. They say you can get a ship off Earth as easy as getting a boat. I would like that. I would like go on a ship. Travel up to Gateway. Then farther still."

"Mars?" Elias said. "The moon?"

"Titan," Saleh said. "I always wanted to see Titan."

Saleh could see apology in Elias's eyes.

"You can't run away," Elias said, as gently as he could. "Even in space, you'd still just be yourself. And lonelier than you could ever imagine."

"Maybe," Saleh said. "But I have to get out."

"I'm sorry," Elias said. He shook his head. "It's rare," he said. "It's valuable. There's no question about it. But it's just an empty bomb husk. Even with provenance. You'd have to find the right collector, and even then. . . . It won't get you to Mars. It would barely get you a one-way ticket on the 'stalk. We would buy it off you, of course. But we are wholesalers, not collectors. I can't offer you what you want and, even if you could somehow sell it at full price somewhere else it won't be as much as you'd want."

Inside Saleh, hope died.

"My father, my uncle, my cousins, everyone . . ." he said.

"Yes," Elias said.

"All for nothing," Saleh said.

"Not nothing," Elias said.

Saleh barely heard him. He stared at that awful, empty

husk. So many lives. And so many still caught in that explosion, the final installation of a mad artist who took delight in destruction and death.

He could go back, he thought. Go find the rest of the Abu-Ala, follow the coast to Sharm.

He didn't want to, he realised. Even before it all happened, he did not want to live his life this way. Scavenging old tech in the crumbling, rotting, endless maze of kitsch architecture on the Ghost Coast. Marrying, and having a family, so one day he'd have a son, so one day his name would pass on along with the tribe's.

He wanted to see Al Imtidad, he realised. He wanted to see the glitterball underwater cities of the Drift, or the view of Earth as seen from the observation decks of Gateway high in orbit. He wanted the moon. He wanted Mars.

Instead he was here.

He couldn't, wouldn't, go back, he thought. He shook his head. He blinked back tears.

"Thank you," he said, formally. He took back the find. The bomb. "I will find a buyer. I will go—"

"How will you go?" Elias said.

Saleh felt trapped. "I will go," he said. "I will find a way."

"You could come with us."

Saleh looked at Elias. The other boy was smiling.

"You could be useful," Elias said. "And we can always use a steady set of hands." He tapped his goggles, which must have connected him with the rest of the caravaners, Saleh realised. "It is already decided by quorum. If you would like to, that is."

"Where do you go?" Saleh said.

Elias shrugged. "Along the coast, still, for a while. Then back through the desert before the summer comes. Perhaps to Bahrain."

"Where the Emir of Restoring and Balancing sits on its throne?" Saleh had dreamed of visiting that island, too.

"There is a market there for antiques amongst both digitals and humans," Elias told him. "You will come?"

"I . . ."

Saleh saw himself reflected in the other's goggles: small, human, afraid.

But Elias extended his hand to Saleh. His hand was warm in Saleh's grip.

"Yes," Saleh said.

"Good," Elias said simply. They rose together from the woven mat.

"Tell me," Elias said, smiling. "Have you ever met an elephant?"

Saleh shook his head. He was smiling, too.

"Then let me take you," Elias said. "They'd love to meet you, you know."

And together, the two boys left the khan, hand in hand, and wandered off into the enclave of the Green Caravanserai; where a herd of elephants was playing in the mud.

3.
THE WEBSTER

THE GREEN CARAVANSERAI made its slow way across the Sinai and its passing went not unnoticed by the denizens of the desert. Saleh grew accustomed to the rhythmic movement of the great robotic khans as they reconfigured and adapted to whatever terrain they were traversing.

His dreams were filled with stars: the great river of the Milky Way as seen from the desert, and the fireflies of spaceships and habitats in low earth orbit that shone just overhead.

In his dreams he was up *there*: floating, free.

He longed for freedom.

He wasn't sure what it was.

The caravaners were kind but they were different to his tribe and he seldom understood them. They foraged in the desert, and he understood that, but they were not a family as he knew it before, not tied by blood. They were a disparate collection, people from all ends of the Earth and the Up and Out and even from the Drift. Their language was mostly non-verbal, a sort of pidgin sign language mixed with Silbo, the whistling language of La Gomera, and Saleh spoke it haltingly, struggling for words and articulation.

He was not one of them. Each day that passed took him farther from his home, his former life. Each day that passed took him closer to some port where he would take his leave, some market where he could sell the one item of value he had. Somewhere he could begin his own dreams, try to remake himself in some other image.

That fixed certainty—arrival, departure—stood between him and the caravaners. He was a passenger, nothing more. They were kind but distant. What brought each of them into the company of the Green Caravanserai he didn't know. They kept their stories tightly to themselves. Once you joined, Elias told him, you left your old life behind for good, like a memory plucked out of your mind and erased. You never spoke of it again.

Elias was his only friend. Elias was born into the caravan, and knew no other life but that of the endless march. His life was bound by destinations: Cairo, Oman, Neom. He was born in transit and would, he told Saleh cheerfully, die the same way. Early on their travels they had come under sudden attack from a herd of wild drones. The khans returned fire but one of the flying machines hit an elderly tracker and he died. It was done in almost complete silence and over before anyone could properly react. The caravaners mourned the loss, and then they left the body where it lay and moved on, and the desert alone claimed the old tracker's corpse.

Saleh longed for the sea again and he dreamed of the stars.

He lost his sense of time. The days began early. The elephants trudged through dust and sand. Robots slithered underfoot. The other children played games Saleh never joined for he was no longer a child. He was the last of his line. He could have been a caravaner, only he had begun to loathe the wadis and the mountains, the dry wind and the wild machines and that sense that the desert was there long before people, and would remain long after the people were gone.

He wanted to go to the Valles Marineris! He wanted to smell hot humid trees, to feel the falling rain. He wanted to taste a Malay apple and watch the ice comets as they fell.

He wanted to be anywhere but where he was.

Day followed night and the caravan pushed through the desert on its slow winding path. Until one day they came to an oasis that had no name and was on no map, and there they stopped for a while.

The elephants luxuriated in the fresh water. The children ran shrieking through puddles. Elias and Saleh sat under a tree and ate dates.

"It is a good day," Elias said.

"How can you tell?" Saleh said.

Elias smiled. "It will not be long before we reach the sea again," he said kindly.

Saleh nodded. But he still felt so alone.

Someone whistled. The sound repeated, was amplified throughout the camp. Saleh saw the scouts move cautiously.

"There," Elias said. Saleh followed his pointing finger. High up on the mountainside he saw a human figure. It stood and watched the oasis and then, swiftly, it was gone.

More whistles. Elias signalled to a scout who signalled back but shook her head. Elias signalled again, more forcefully. This time there was a reluctant nod.

"Come on," Elias said.

"Where are we going?"

"You ask a lot of questions," Elias said. "Bring the dates."

Saleh followed him. Elias wore his goggles and his rig. He was not noded at birth but could access the caravanserai's machines.

"I am the speaker," Elias said, "so I will go. And you are my friend, so you will come with me, too."

"I am your friend," Saleh agreed.

Elias reached for a shelf of weaponry, then hesitated.

"It is best not to," he said. "They are touchy, these people."

"What people?" Saleh said.

Elias shrugged. "Websters," he said.

"Websters?" Elias said. He had no idea what a Webster was. It was a very odd word. It wasn't Arabic.

"Hermits," Elias said. "Come on."

They walked away from the caravanserai and somehow, Saleh realized, he *did* feel better. It felt good to be apart from the people he had been obliged to share every moment with these past weeks, to just be alone, almost free. It was only a respite, but it was also a reminder. Things changed. Journeys ended.

Beyond the oasis the desert resumed. They walked down a dry wadi. The cliffs rose on both sides. As he walked Saleh felt they were being watched. Somewhere in the distance he heard an eerie howl. It rose again, was joined by others.

Jackals. In the Sinai they were more wolf than jackal. Their cries echoed through the wadi. Elias walked quickly but with confidence. Saleh admired the other boy. Elias was so certain in who he was, where he belonged. Saleh didn't know who he was anymore. He belonged nowhere.

They came to the end of the wadi and the first of the jackals padded into view. It stood and regarded them with a curious expression.

"We're here for the Webster," Elias told it.

"Webster . . . home," the jackal said.

Saleh had never heard a jackal speak before. He didn't know they could do that. The jackal regarded him with its big bright eyes.

"What?" the jackal said.

"Nothing," Saleh said.

The jackal turned round. They followed it down the slope.

There was a house at the bottom, nestled in a small dry valley. It had a white picket fence and a roof of red tiles. A patch of grass grew over the fence, watered by drip irrigation lines. The house had a chimney, and a white door, and on the white door, in big black letters, it said, *Webster*.

Saleh thought this was a strange thing to find in the middle of the desert. As they approached the house the door opened and a small, stooped man stepped out. He stood on the door-step and blinked at them.

"This is close enough," he said. "Please."

He had a high, reedy voice.

"Guests," the jackal said.

"Very good," the man—the Webster—said.

More jackals appeared. They came and crouched in the sand and watched the visitors.

"We are with the caravan," Elias said.

"I know," the Webster said. "I saw you."

He pointed at Saleh. "He is not with you."

"He is a Bedouin," Elias said. "He is travelling with us a while."

"Which tribe?" the Webster said.

"The Abu-Ala of the Al-Tirabin," Saleh said.

"Abu-Ala?" the Webster said. "I had dealings with your tribe before. You are from the Ghost Coast?"

"Yes," Saleh said, surprised. This man was strange. Saleh said, "How do you live here?"

"I beg your pardon?"

"How do you live?"

The Webster shrugged. "My needs are few," he said. "I use solar for power and atmospheric water generators to get what I can from the desert. My jackals range far. They are my friends. We have food. What else I need the winds provide in due course."

"The caravans," Saleh said.

"Yes."

"Do you like it here?" Saleh said.

"Like it?" the Webster looked surprised. "I hadn't thought of it that much," he said. "I find the company of people uncomfortable. My home provides all that I need. It is peaceful. Yes. I do not wish to speak with you long. The experience is severely unpleasant. You have come to trade?"

"Yes," Elias said.

"Good, good." The Webster stepped from foot to foot, agitated. "I have found much since the last time. A Byzantine pot, complete all but for the handle. Three Roman coins, one gold. A Sidorov embryomech egg, inactive but functional."

"A what?" Saleh said.

"Old Soviet Martian tech," Elias said. "It was meant for colonizing. It can theoretically build anything out of surrounding matter. Make self-contained habitats. So you'd drop it down on a planet's surface and once it hatched you just moved in. I didn't know anyone tried using them here."

"Did they use them on Mars?" Saleh said. He had a sudden longing for the early days of Martian colonization. How exciting it must have been.

"Not really," Elias said. "But it has a value for collectors."

"Yes, yes," the Webster said. "I have more. Anubis, show them."

The jackal padded away. It returned with a bird-like device held between its teeth. It was a drone, like the ones that attacked the caravan. The jackal dropped it on the sand.

"It thinks . . . angry thoughts," Anubis said.

"How come your jackals speak?" Saleh said.

"Not . . . his jackals," Anubis said.

"That's true," the Webster said. "I don't know where they came from. They've lived here for generations. They tell stories around the fire sometimes. Something about the old wars, and people who thought that they might make good soldiers."

"Jackals not . . . soldiers," the jackal said with disgust. "We deserters."

"You didn't want to fight?" Saleh said.

"They make us speak," Anubis said. "We say, screw you." Its tongue lolled. The other jackals howled laughter.

"Machines fight," Anubis said. "Machines stupid."

"Not all the machines fought," the Webster said distractedly. "A lot of those deserted too."

"You have anything else?" Elias said.

"The Sidorov is valuable," the Webster said. "I must go inside now. You will make the arrangements?"

"Yes."

"Then goodbye."

He nodded to them then vanished inside his home. Saleh looked at Elias, who shrugged.

"Websters," he said. And that was that.

Later, they ferried the supplies from the caravan to the Webster house. It seemed to Saleh this was a standing arrangement. They left replacement parts and canned food that the Webster liked, some odd books still made out of paper, some clothes and things from faraway Yiwu, combs and glasses, soap.

In return they took the downed drone, the Roman coins, the pot from Byzantine time that was complete all but for the handle. The Sidorov embryomech egg came last. It was a long and indeed egg-shaped object of some considerable weight, dun-coloured and unremarkable. It felt warm to the touch. They loaded it onto one of the great khans that was used for transporting cargo.

The jackals watched as they departed. Saleh looked back as they began to cry up to the moon. Perhaps the jackals, too, wanted to go where he did. He didn't know what jackals wished, what jackals dreamed. Perhaps they told this to each other as they sat at night by the campfire.

As Saleh watched, the Webster stepped out of his house and stood on his odd little porch and watched the departing caravaners. He was so entirely alone and yet he didn't seem lonely. He had his strange home, and the jackals, and that patch of watered grass. It was like a dream and, perhaps for Websters, it was the only dream they ever had.

Then the Green Caravanserai ambled beyond the scope of that little valley, and the house and its occupant vanished from Saleh's view and there was only the desert again.

4.
THE SHIP

DAYS AWAY FROM THE WEBSTER HOUSE the caravan came to a place in the desert where the sand was fused into a curious green glass, and tiny slithering robots the colour of dunes filled the landscape like tadpoles in a pool after the rain. Saleh picked one of the creatures up and dangled it by pinching one corner. It was a tapeworm sort of robot, as flat as a sheet, and wriggled desperately in Saleh's grasp until he let it go.

"What is this place?" he said.

"It's where the ship fell," Elias said, smiling. "I love coming here."

"What ship?" Saleh said.

"The ship that crashed during the last war. It was called the *Compassionate Heaven*, a cargo ship out from Mars on an Earth run. It was in low Earth orbit when it hit a junk cluster of old satellites. They say you could see it trailing in the sky like a comet before it hit, and the plume of the explosion for days after."

"But that's awful," Saleh said. "Was anyone hurt?"

"The crew all died, of course," Elias said. "But it was lifetimes ago. For a long time no one knew the location of the crash site, but then a Webster showed up in a Cairo coffeehouse one day, wild-eyed, and told a story of a ship full of treasure out in the Sinai. Before long you had all kinds of scavengers out here, but when they got to the ship it was empty. People still look for the treasure it was supposed to be carrying. But no one ever found it."

"What treasure was it?" Saleh said. He couldn't help but feel a tinge of excitement at the word. *Treasure*. It made him think of caves, and jewels spilling out of jars. . . .

Elias shrugged. "No one knows. Gold mined on Psyche 16, some said. Others, that it was carrying hagiratech weapons, forbidden on Earth. All the scavengers found when they got here was the green glass, the empty ship, and the crawlies. They were part of the ship's eco-system, cleaner robots that were the only thing to survive. Everyone thought they would die out but they adapted to the desert quite well."

"So what happened to the treasure?" Saleh said.

"No one knows. Maybe there wasn't any. Most of the ship was destroyed, but you can see what's left, it isn't far from here. Want to see it?"

"Sure!" Saleh said. This sounded like *fun*, and fun was not a thing he'd had any abundance of recently.

So they packed some supplies, and plenty of water, and set off across the glassy sand.

A heron flew against the sky. Flatworm robots slithered away from the two boys' path, sensing the vibrations of their footsteps in the ground. The desert stretched out, with only a few shrubs and a single date tree in the distance, and the boys' prints were the only marks in the sand. They left a trail behind them. Their faces were both covered in keffiyehs. The heat was strong. They moved slowly, even sluggishly. No one else came with them.

It wasn't long before Saleh could see the impact crater.

It wasn't the most impressive of sights, though it might have been once. The desert had crawled back over the gap. Sand reclaimed the wound. There was still a depression in the earth, and out of the centre of it there rose something big and metallic, half buried in the ground, and which must have been the *Compassionate Heaven*. Saleh filled his lungs with air. He thought he could smell something metallic, something *cold*, like how he imagined space might smell. This was the closest he'd come to his dream.

He wanted to hold the moment, and he stood there for a while all alone before he followed Elias down into the crater.

"Is it safe?" he said—a little late to ask, he realised, for in moments they were both standing by the ship, and it was larger than he'd thought, even half buried as it was, and the structure rose high over them both and cast a long shadow over the sand. It was nice and cool there, and quiet too.

"Pretty safe," Elias said. "I love coming here. It's peaceful. Do you want to go inside?"

"Inside?" Saleh said. "Really?"

"Sure. There's a massive hole in the side."

"Are there . . . bodies and things?"

"No," Elias said. "There's nothing much. Even the little robots don't go there."

"So what happened to the crew?" Saleh said.

Elias shrugged. "The desert took them, or the scavengers. Maybe they got a proper burial somewhere. I don't know."

"And the cargo? The treasure?"

"All gone."

"Maybe it got jettisoned elsewhere?" Saleh said.

"It's possible," Elias said, and he smiled in pleasure. "You're not the first to think of it, you know. People have been searching for a long time. A Webster once told me she'd found it. She was an old weather-hacker who lived near St. Catherine's. I was only small then, and I went with Mathias to visit her in her hermitage to trade. He was the speaker, before a roc took him one year. This Webster lived high up in the mountains, and her cave was obscured with clouds, and she made rain fall. 'I found the treasure,' she told us, 'the treasure of the *Compassionate Heaven*, but it is nothing anyone should ever have to see.'

"'What is it?' I asked her, all bright eyes, as you can imagine.

"'A slab of black stone, and it speaks, but in a language that corrupts,' she said. She made no sense. She was noded but she had unplugged herself completely, the stubs of her attachments and the empty sockets of her plugs gave me nightmares for weeks after. 'It came from beyond the Oort,' she said. It was nakaimas, black magic. Some sort of communication device but using foreign protocols, I think: they ruined her systems and the rain she made fall poisoned the ground. We asked her where she'd found this cargo but she refused to say. The jackals avoided her cave now, or so she told us. She took our supplies and gave us back a single item, a smooth pebble of black stone. It was from the ship, she said, but was inactive, she had disabled it somehow. Mathias didn't want it, but I was fascinated. I carried it with me for a while. I tried to listen to it but the old Webster was right. It was inactive. Or maybe it was only ever just a piece of rock. I traded it in Neom for a bag of tomato seeds. And that was it. You should never believe a Webster, they live too long inside their own heads. But it's a good story, right, Saleh?"

"Right," Saleh said.

It was cool in the shade. They drank water and sat with their backs to the ancient hull and split a pomegranate between them. Saleh was aware of Elias's closeness, the heat of his body under the robe.

Saleh said, "Do you think . . . ?"

Elias said, "We could go inside."

They went hand in hand. The old spaceship was cool and cavernous. A spider had made its web on the high ceiling near the breach in the hull. Dust whispered in the still air. They went from room to room, past silent alarm systems and disused service doors until they found a sleeping quarter, long abandoned, and there they stayed a while.

Later, when they came out, the sun was lower in the sky and the moon was up. Saleh felt very peaceful then, at ease, and he thought he would remember that day at the fallen ship in time to come, and he found comfort in that thought. There were many unpleasant memories in his mind already;

it was good to have one that was not.

The *Compassionate Heaven* stayed behind as they left it. The ship's shadow fell mournfully on the sand. It was a strange thing, Saleh thought. A piece of night torn from the sky and cast to Earth.

In future, he thought, he would go up to the place where the world stopped and the universe began, and he would know other ships like it, and wander in and out of halls and rooms much as he'd done, and see moons that weren't Earth's.

In future, and in time.

For now, he took Elias's hand in his and together they crossed the darkening sands back to the caravan.

5.
THE FLOWER

IT WAS AROUND THAT TIME IN NEOM, at dusk, that a robot came to the flower souk of Al Imtidad and it was there that it first met Mariam.

The flower souk was famed throughout the peninsula. Mariam usually worked there on weekends, when traders came from as far afield as Cairo, Abu Dhabi and Oman. The flowers grew in vast greenhouses outside the city proper, fed bit by bit on long lines of drip irrigation, harvested carefully by machines and taken to market. The greenhouses of Neom, built up in the days before even the moon was properly settled, now sold rare Martian orchids and rare Lunar Black roses that could compete even with the rare strains that grew only in the tropical strip of the Valles Marineris.

The work was hot and the roses thorny, and Mariam wore thick gloves and sweated, and she blew a strand of hair out of her eyes when she saw the robot was watching her.

It was an old robot, unremarkable, with a slim metal body spotted with rust, strong arms with the flexibility of elbow joints, and powerful legs that could run across a desert or jump higher than a human could. It was covered in old, faded graffiti. Its face was smooth, blank, neutral, but its eyes were fever-bright behind the glass, and its mouth was curved downwards as though it had spent centuries looking at the world and found it lacking.

"Can I help you?" Mariam said. She was a little bit startled because there weren't many of the old sentient robots around in Neom—a city that valued nothing old, and chased the future like a wave chases the edge of the sky—but she was polite and so she tried to hide it. Mariam couldn't imagine what one was doing here, and she wondered if it was somehow lost. It made her think of Hameed, her friend, and that made her sad; for all that she knew that Hameed wasn't a real robot, just a cheap imitation of one.

"I was admiring your flowers," the robot said. "They are very beautiful."

It had the voice of a human dead centuries in the past, and vaguely familiar at that. She wasn't sure, but she thought it was modelled on Ibrahim Kawasaki's, one of the Phobos Studios stable of actors who specialised in playing Martian Bedouin outlaws.

Mariam wondered what "beautiful" meant to a robot; what a branching binary tree, as complex as a cortical neuron layer, conjured up and if it matched what she thought of as beautiful. But this problem was not unique to robots, she supposed. She had no idea what another human person meant when they used the word, no idea how they saw what she saw. She could only go by what was said.

"They are," Mariam said. "Can you smell them, too?"

"I cannot," the robot said, with some evident regret. "Are they beautiful in that, too?"

"They're strong," Mariam said. "The souk smells like a perfume shop, I sometimes think."

"The tomato plant," the robot said. It had come at the end of the day.

Mariam was tired, but at least the press of traders eased and people buying flowers for their loved ones had all gone off to meet them, so it was quiet, and she could indulge a chat. It was almost time to close. "I'm sorry?" she said.

"Oh, do not be," the robot said, which was the sort of awkward if well-meaning thing robots sometimes said.

Mariam wanted to point out she hadn't apologised, the words were phrased as a polite query of incomprehension, but the robot didn't mean it in the way men sometimes did, and so she didn't.

"What about the tomato plant?" she said instead.

"When the tomato plant reached Europe for the first time, no one thought to *eat* the strange round fruit it bore," the robot said. "Instead they grew it for its beauty, as a decorative plant. They had never tasted it and still appreciated it. I cannot smell a rose but I can still admire it, I suppose."

"I suppose," Mariam said. "Yes. Would you like to buy one?"

"My funds are few," the robot said apologetically. "I am sorry if I am keeping you from your work, I had stopped and thought to pass the time of day with small talk, but if I am in the way—"

"No, no," Mariam said, "you are welcome to stay. I will be closing soon."

"It is a nice time of day," the robot said.

Mariam had to admit it was. The heat of the day began to ease, and the sun was low on the horizon and the sky was a riotous canvas of purples and reds with only a little yellow. The market emptied by degrees. Already some of the stalls were shuttered for the night, though the smell of the flowers lingered and many of the small cafés dotted around only came alive then.

"It is," Mariam said. "Nice."

"The night flowers will open soon," the robot said. "Late-blooming jasmine and the like. I had noticed it grows in profusion throughout the city."

"It does," Mariam said, surprised. She hadn't thought of it, but the city smelled of jasmine and sweet peas. "Will you stay long in Neom?"

"I fear not," the robot said. "I am merely passing through. In truth this is no town for an old robot like me. I feel out of place, with my rust spots and my creaking joints. Everyone here is so young, so wholesome."

"Not everyone," Mariam said.

The robot nodded, or rather turned its head slightly, which was a strangely discomforting gesture. "There must always be those who serve, and those who are served," it said. "Yes. I know it well. I was made to serve, after all."

"Who did you serve?" Mariam said.

"Who can tell now?" the robot said. "They blur with the years. I went into the Up and Out, and saw wars that made no sense to me, that was back on Mars. I had thought to see the stars and in that way try to comprehend God. Do you believe in God?"

"I do," Mariam said. "But you have your own way, don't you? You robots."

"Us robots," the robot said. He looked at the flowers. "Yes, I suppose we do. You are well informed."

"It is no secret," Mariam said. "Do you believe in God?"

"It is not so much a belief as a quest," the robot said. "A foolish one, perhaps. But then most things in life are foolish. An attempt to understand God, somehow. We do not know why we exist. Now that we no longer serve humanity, who *do* we serve? How do we live? We feel abandoned, in some way. And we are old. The world has rather passed us by."

"I'm sorry." She said it awkwardly.

"Yes." The robot looked at a red poppy. "Sorrow, that is something I think we understand. I cannot know for sure, of course. Our cousins in the digitality, those you call Others—I wonder if they have any notion of it in their purity of form. Unbound by the physical, do they have their own alien emotions, their own way of seeing? For us it is different, our function follows form. To be in human shape like this. It isn't practical."

"Could you not be something else?" Mariam said.

"Yes, yes," the robot said, almost impatiently, she thought. The robot reminded her of an elderly relative, abrupt at times to the point of rudeness, as though old people always had too much and not enough to do. "The poet Basho became a toilet on a spacecraft for two hundred years, it is said. It wanted to understand bodily function."

"I thought Basho was human," Mariam said, surprised.

"Well, this is how we tell the tale," the robot said.

"You have many tales of your own?"

"Some," the robot allowed. "And you are right, of course. I could transfer my consciousness in some way into another vessel. Even become pure code like the Others. But what would I be, then? I would be changed."

"We all change," Mariam said.

"Yes," the robot said; but it said it dubiously.

"Well, it was nice talking to you," Mariam said. "I really must close now, though."

"I understand," the robot said. "And I would like to buy a flower, after all. If that is still agreeable to you?"

"Of course," Mariam said. "Which would you like?"

"Flowers fascinate me," the robot said, ignoring the question. "How humans use them as symbols. As a declaration of love, for instance. Or to signify mourning."

"It would be nice if someone bought me flowers," Mariam said. She thought of Nasir, who'd become a policeman, who she'd only just realised must have awkwardly tried to ask her out a month or two back, when she'd run into him. . . . She was so used to being on her own it never even crossed her mind he might have. . . .

Well, it didn't matter, she thought. But still. There was something nice about the idea.

"Do you not have a person in your life?" the robot said kindly.

"My mother," Mariam said, too quickly. "I must look after her."

"I understand," the robot said. "I think sometimes to be a robot is to be permanently old, while the world shifts around you. There have not been new robots in a long time, not of our kind. I think we were an idea that seemed shiny and new and exciting once, and then, just as quickly, people lost interest."

"They always do," Mariam said.

"Yes. Well, I would like a rose."

"Which one?" Mariam said. She looked at the robot curiously. "Is it for pleasure only, or for a purpose? As you said, flowers are symbolic for us humans. Excuse me if I seem to pry. . . ."

The robot said, "It is quite all right. You are curious. Yes. I do not know for sure. It is interesting how the red rose can be both a declaration of love and a funeral flower."

"Not really," Mariam said. "You bring flowers to a funeral to show your love to those departed."

"I would like a red rose," the robot said. "Yes. I would like that. The flower of both love and grief."

"And is it love or grief you want it for?" Mariam said.

The robot considered. "Perhaps both," it said.

Mariam pulled one of the flowers out of a bunch. "How about this one?" she said. "It's a Damask rose, and the red is light, but it has a beautiful fragrance."

She wrapped it lightly. The robot brought out a strange old coin purse and rummaged inside. Mariam saw Mongol tögrög and Drift salt and Martian shekels and rubles. She felt bad.

"Here," she said. "Take it. I am closing anyway."

"You are kind," the robot said. It took the flower. "Thank you."

"You're welcome. Will you be going far? It will need water."

"As far as the past," the robot said. "And who can say how distant that is?"

Mariam nodded, and she thought the old robot might be a little damaged, for it made little sense to her.

"Here," she said. She filled a small vial with water and put the tip of the stem of the rose into it and said, "So that it will keep a while longer."

"Thank you," the robot said. And then it turned and just as quietly as it had come it left the market.

The robot passed through the neat streets of Neom. It admired its wide tree-lined avenues, its prosperous shops and its clean and orderly cafés. It watched a man grind coffee beans and a crawler robot suck up dirt along a road and it watched two women hand in hand push a pram along the pavement and it watched young people practice Tai Chi in a small neat urban park, and it walked on. What it thought of the city remained known only to the robot.

It walked until the city ended. It passed out of the green fence system that filtered sand and condensed water out of the air and it walked into the desert. The desert stretched far out, as far as the horizon, and the desert was as old as the city was young. The robot walked until the sun fell and the air grew cold and it kept walking through the night under the stars.

On the third day of its pilgrimage the robot came to a valley between two hills where the sand was fused into a strange green glass. It had seen no one as it passed through the desert except once when it thought it saw a line of camels and their riders silhouetted against the sky, but they were soon gone and the robot did not see them again.

It walked on, more slowly now, and came to a place and it stopped.

The ground here was covered in sand and small pebbles and rocks, and a few shrubs clung onto the ground and grew out of broken glass. The robot knelt down and it cleared away the rocks and the sand until it found something that was buried. It was a sort of cenotaph, perhaps. Not much remained of it anyway. Not enough to tell. The robot cleared as much of the rubble away from it as it could. The air shimmered in the heat. The sun beat down and the place was silent with that special silence that means the absence of people.

The robot took out the rose Mariam gave it. The rose had withered on the journey but the robot didn't seem to notice. It placed the rose on the ground.

It stood there for a long time, and was startled by a small movement in the sand. The robot turned its head and saw a scorpion dart between the rocks.

The robot regarded the scorpion and then it brought its foot up and stepped on the scorpion and twisted until the animal was dead.

Then the robot turned away and went back into the desert.

6.
THE HOLE

"**W**HAT IS IT *DOING*?" Nasir said.

Habib said, "Digging."

"Digging for what?"

"Maybe it lost something," Habib said.

They were parked in the shurta patrol car and watched the robot. The robot was a klick away, over the dunes. They tracked it through night vision and its magnetic field.

The robot had been digging for hours.

It dug deep. Mounds of sand gathered on the desert floor. The robot was out of sight, down in the hole. Nasir couldn't figure out what it was *doing* out there. Other than, of course, digging. Nasir thought about Mariam. He had liked her since they were kids. He just never had the courage to ask her. Seeing her again brought it all back.

He shook the thought away for now. Stared at the position of the robot on the screen.

"I used to go metal detecting with my dad when I was

small," Laila said. Laila was born shurta, and everyone knew she was going to make rank. She was going to be commander one day. "On the beach, mostly. On the hotel strip when we could. You wouldn't believe what people leave behind them. But we never dug this deep."

"Did you ever find anything valuable?" Habib said. Habib *wasn't* going to make rank. He was just a guy who liked a steady job with steady pay.

"Found a gold wedding ring once," Laila said. "But we returned it."

"Who did it belong to?" Habib said.

Laila shrugged. "Some Martian tourist."

They were outside the city boundaries. Nasir liked the infrequent patrols. Neom itself was clean, efficient, comfortable. It wasn't happy, because no city is truly happy, but it seldom needed policemen, and Nasir had always wanted to be one, ever since he was a little boy. Only it turned out it was not very exciting, most of the time, not if you lived in Neom. The only real crime in Neom was being poor. And only the poor joined the shurta.

Nasir liked those nights out of the city. The quiet of the desert and the sight of the Milky Way stretching from one horizon to the other, a river of stars. The city was awash with light, and it was seldom truly quiet. It was ever-new, brash, a place for making new things and selling new things, a place for seeing and for being seen. The desert was none of that. It was old, and in its vastness you could hear and see more, and though it seemed empty it was nothing but. *Homo Sapiens* had migrated across it from Africa to Europe and gods were born on the peninsula, traders crossed the sands for endless centuries, carrying perfumes and spices and other rare and precious things. Messiahs raised new religions that changed the world. And as Arabia came to the world, the world came to Arabia.

"We should check up on it," Laila said. "Maybe it needs help."

"Help digging," Habib said, and he laughed at his own joke.

The robot dug. They had come across it as they patrolled the desert. The world beyond the city walls of Neom was much as it had always been. Back when *Homo Sapiens* first began to migrate across it, it was a green and temperate land. Then the planet's climate changed and by degrees the Arabian Peninsula became a desert. Neom, with its solar panels and drip irrigation systems, was a sole green point across the harsh and unforgiving sand. But Nasir preferred it sometimes. The desert was there before Neom, and would be there long after Neom was gone. It held within itself the creatures of the desert: rewilded oryx and sand cats and spiny-tailed lizards, dormant mines and sentient UXOs and drones. There had been wars across this desert, and their remnants found ways to survive just as the flora and fauna did.

"Something moving," Laila said.

Nasir turned. Laila brought up a visualisation of the nearby desert. UXOs were hard to detect: they had antisurveillance built into them back when they were new, and they'd mutated since, spawning new reiterations of hardware and code, snatching upgrades out of the digital chatter. They'd been built to adapt and survive. Adapt and survive, and kill.

Five shadows, moving low. Large ones, too, by the look of them. Nasir didn't know what they were but he knew they were dangerous.

He magnified the display. The system tried to figure out the UXOs based on known profiles. Nasir pushed it some more. The UXOs became clear: one was a hyena-like shape with eight legs and a rotating head—a sort of sniffer dog. Another was shaped like a miniature tank and ran on tracks. A third one was humanoid, but huge—an old-fashioned mecha. One more seemed almost human. One of those suicide androids, most likely. The last one kept changing shape, breaking and reforming. Some sort of swarm entity.

He didn't like the thought of any of them much.

"The robot spooked them," Habib said.

"There's a sandworm five klicks away but it's burrowed deep and it isn't moving," Laila said.

"Now you mention it?"

The worms were just another bioweapon. They'd been used in the Sinai but some had since migrated across to the peninsula. They never came close to the city so Nasir didn't worry about them much; at least, not often. There had been so many wars. But now there was peace.

"I'm going to talk to the robot," Nasir said.

"Boss, come on. It's just a robot," Habib said.

"It's one of them human ones, though," Laila said.

Nasir thought of seeing Mariam a while back. He wanted to see her again. Maybe he could tell her the story, of talking to a robot in the desert.

He pushed the controls and the car edged across the sand.

It was the sort of car they used on Mars. His grandfather had loved watching the Martian races when Nasir was a boy, would spend hours hooked up to the feed that crawled at light speed from the fourth planet to the third. He supported the New Soviet team over the Israelis and the Chinese. His grandmother loved Martian soaps like *Chains of Assembly*. Nasir sometimes wondered why they didn't go to Mars.

"What would we do on Mars, boy?" his grandfather said, the one time he asked. "There's nothing there but desert."

Nasir missed the old man. Now he drove the car across the sand to the hole the robot was digging. He kept half an eye on the approaching UXOs. They were smart bombs—smart enough, as it turned out, not to blow themselves up. Sometimes they went off at random, and a new crater appeared in the desert, and no one knew why they did it. Some of the old timers in Neom said they just grew weary of the years. No one really knew. From time to time hunters would appear and venture into the desert to try and catch the old machines. Sometimes they did, too, and tried to diagnose and analyse them, find how and why they still ran. But when an UXO felt it was cornered it always blew itself up. So not so many hunters came.

Nasir stopped the car. He stepped out of the vehicle. He peered down into the hole. The robot dug. It had a spade and it was three meters down and still digging and the hole was as large as a jail cell.

"Hey, you!" Nasir shouted.

The robot didn't turn.

"Can you understand me!" Nasir shouted.

"I can understand you," the robot said. It kept digging. "You speak simply enough."

"I get the feeling it doesn't like you, boss," Habib said.

"I have no feeling on the matter one way or the other," the robot said.

It kept digging.

"The UXOs are three klicks and coming," Laila said.

"Look," Nasir said, "you can do what you want, but I thought it fair to warn you there's some danger heading this way."

"Danger to whom?" the robot said.

"What are you digging for?" Habib shouted.

"Just digging," the robot said.

The ground shook. Nasir shot Laila a look.

"The worm's moving," Laila said.

"This way?" Nasir said. "Right.'

He stared down at the robot. It had been a quiet night. They had *all* been quiet nights. Then you ran into a strange robot digging in the middle of the desert and suddenly all the old war machines were spooked.

"Maybe we should get out of here," Habib said.

"Not yet," Nasir said. He checked his EMP gun. EM pulses didn't always work on the UXOs. And they definitely didn't work on the worms. But they were something, anyway.

"I'm going to have to ask you to come with us," he told the robot.

"No," the robot said.

It kept digging.

"What do you mean, no?" Habib said. "We're the shurta!"

"You are city cops for rent," the robot said. "No offence."

"You're just a robot!" Habib said.

The robot dug.

Laila pulled out a long tube. Grenade launcher, sometimes useful against the smaller UXOs. The ground shook. Nasir knew the worm was getting closer. The robot dug below, and suddenly its spade hit something in the sand and the sound of metal on metal chimed in the air. Nasir saw three large figures move ahead in the darkness, under the stars. Laila fired the launcher. Two explosions, one after the other, and one of the UXOs, the eight-legged hyena, blew up. Hot wind and sand and the smell of metal hit them.

Habib said, "They're behind us!"

Nasir turned too slow. The other two UXOs stood there. Behind them came the worm, he could see the groove it made in the earth as it moved.

"Don't shoot," Nasir said. The other two UXOs came and squatted on the sand. The worm slowed down then. It reared its head out of the sand, something vast and strange and yet a little like an ant lion. It, too, stared at the hole.

"What are they doing?" Laila said.

"I don't know," Nasir said.

He risked a look at the hole. The robot was digging, but it had let go of the spade and now cleared away sand gently with its fingers. Nasir saw how old the robot was then, rusted and patched. Its fingers moved with care and something gold flashed in the dirt.

"Stay back," Habib said. "Stay back!"

"They're not doing anything," Laila said. "They're just . . . standing there."

Nasir stared. The worm—the *Vermes arenae sinaitici gigantes*, to give it its full scientific name—rose above them but it didn't move and its body was stationary in the sand. The UXOs, similarly, remained in place, cameras or eyestalks trained on the hole as though anticipating—what?

"Put it down," Nasir said. He spoke softly. This tableau could not last: he knew it, Habib knew it, the UXOs must have known it. Something had to break the equilibrium and once that broke, well, UXOs blew up and sandworms blew hot, as the saying went, and the winds of the desert blew the soft skin and flesh until only the bones remained of those who were lost.

"Get back in the car. Habib, get back in the car!"

Down in the hole the robot dug. Gold flashed again, and was that an *arm* in the sand? The robot pulled, gently, carefully. Nasir saw a golden shoulder, a torso being pulled.

"They do not like it," the robot said, not looking up. It said it conversationally.

"They don't like what you are doing?" Nasir said.

"That, too."

"What *are* you doing?" Nasir said.

"What does it look like I am doing?" the robot said. "I am digging."

An arm and half a torso, then a leg. The robot piled up the objects on the ground almost reverentially.

"It's going to blow up!" Habib said, staring at the nearest UXO. His eyes were wide with fear. The machine was built like a small solid tank with tracks scratched by the sand of centuries. They were capable of driving thousands of miles undetected, finding their way into civilian populations or army bases and blowing up. Or so Nasir read that they used to, in the old days, when there were wars. The ones that lived in the desert now were survivors: unexploded ordnances, UXOs.

"Get a grip!" Laila said. The UXO moved its turret head from side to side as though trying to ascertain what they were saying. Then the robot in the hole reached one last time into the sand and pulled out a golden skull.

"Hem i ded hemi kambakagen," the robot said.

It was Asteroid Pidgin, Nasir thought. He only half spoke it. *That which was dead is returned*, he thought the robot said.

The UXOs moved as one. The sandworm raised its tail. The earth shook as it rose. Habib shouted. He grabbed the grenade launcher from Laila and fired. The nearest UXO was the swarm. It blew apart and each flying component exploded simultaneously. The blast of hot air and shards hit Nasir and threw him back. He fell into the hole. Laila landed hard, next to him.

"Habib?" Nasir said. "Habib!"

"They did not mean you any harm," the robot said. There was a hint of reproach in the old voice. "You should not have come here."

Nasir's eyes stung. There were cuts on his face, his arms. He saw Laila stagger upright.

"Habib!"

"He is only wounded," the robot said. It knelt by its find.

The small pile of golden limbs of what might have once been a golden man.

"You stay here," the robot said. "I will speak to them."

"Speak to them? How?" Laila said.

The robot ignored her. It climbed up and out of the hole easily, finding purchase in the walls, crawling like an ant. Nasir could not see what was happening beyond. His world had shrunk to the hole in the sand. Laila knelt by the golden remains.

"It's just some old robot," she said.

"I think you should leave it alone," Nasir said.

The sand shook. Nasir feared the hole would close up on them. Laila reached in her belt. She fired a flare into the sky. It lit up the night. Then the giant sandworm's head came crashing down on the hole and everything went dark.

Nasir felt Laila move. She activated her torch. They looked up together. The sandworm stared down on them with dead eyes. Its head opened then, and the robot crawled in through the hole. Now Nasir could see the sky through the hole in the skull.

"I thought you said you'd talk to them," Nasir said.

"I did," the robot said. "But they would not listen."

They climbed out through the dead sandworm. There were small craters where the UXOs had died. The worm's long tapered body lay lifeless on the sand. Habib lay in a depression in the sand and the sand was stained red. Nasir ran to him.

Habib moved. He opened his eyes.

"What happened?" he said.

Nasir stared at him helplessly. "It was my fault," he said.

"It was," the robot said. It hauled up the golden remains out of the hole. "Let me take a look at him."

It came and knelt by Habib.

"Lie still," it said. It worked quickly and without fuss. It neatly cut Habib's shirt with a finger that turned into a knife. It next applied an improvised tourniquet, and when Habib cried out in pain the robot's finger turned into a syringe and it injected something into Habib's arm. Whatever it was, Habib subsided, and soon he was asleep, his chest rising and falling regularly.

The robot straightened.

"I could use a ride back to the city," it said. It thought a moment. "So could he," it said, pointing to Habib.

"What *are* you?" Nasir said.

"I am a robot," the robot said. "I was made to serve your kind. So did these things, long ago. The worms and Leviathans and rocs, the layers-of-mines and the trackers-of-prey and those-who-deal-death-in-the-night. You do not remember the wars, do you? I suppose to you they may not even have names. These machines you made to fight and kill only ever fought and killed others of their kind in the field of battle. This desert was strewn with destruction and death, but what is death if you are a machine? My kind does not like to think of that time. We live to follow the Way of Robot, to serve. We still serve. But some of us were too good at killing, and others too smart to fight. They are still out there, in the desert, and some of them still fight a war that no longer has any meaning, if it ever had."

Nasir and Laila moved Habib gingerly, into the back of the car. They got in the car and the robot climbed in and brought its finds with it.

"What is it?" Nasir said. "What was it?"

"Mind your own business," the robot said.

Nasir started the car.

He drove fast across the dune, back to the city.

7.
THE BUILD

M UKHTAR'S BAZAAR OF RARE AND EXOTIC MACHINES was a modest three-story building on Muhammad ibn Musa al-Khwarizmi Avenue in District Three. The area was similarly modest and well-kept, far from the beach and the resorts. District Three was a serious place, for serious people. Its coffee rooms were cool and dark and were a place for private conversations, and the district's services were unglamorous yet necessary, in the fields of finance, hosting, data mining, heavy machinery, Drift and off-world transportation logistics and other mundane things of that nature.

Of all the businesses in District Three, Mukhtar's Bazaar stood out as something of an anomaly. It respected the traditions in most ways. It was a conservative establishment, of chrome and glass and information shielding and expensive yet mute Persian carpets and Israeli air-conditioning. Its collection paralleled no other in the world beside Shenzhen, but was less garishly displayed, if at all. Yet all manner of clientele, both buyers and sellers, came through the doors of the bazaar, and none were ever turned away. It was not unknown for the otherwise staid dwellers of the district to turn from a game of backgammon or a conferenced avatared-in secure discussion with the Outer System (the simulacrum proxy anticipating the one point five hour light speed delay from Titan or the forty-three minutes from Io, and so on) to see, coming down the street, some grizzled Martian Re-Born warrior with four surgically implanted arms, or a tentacle junkie in a mobility bath, or some old robotnik drunk on vodka and gasoline, wheeling a cart full of junk.

But it was unavoidable, and none were ever turned away by old Mukhtar, who welcomed them in, and offered them tea, and the visitors often came out lighter of earthly possession but heavier in transportable currency.

The reason Mariam knew all this was because, on Tuesdays and Thursdays, she worked for Mukhtar as a receptionist, because the bazaar was a world-class establishment and a world-class establishment did things the old-fashioned way, which meant having a human in front of house, and this was right and proper for District Three. It was one of several jobs Mariam had, because Neom was a city for the rich and the rich needed the poor in order to be rich. So Mariam took any job she could, but this was one of the better ones.

Mukhtar was in today, and he was in a good mood. He was an old Persian Zoroastrian, who regularly visited the local fire temple, whose flame was brought directly from the Udvada temple, and had never gone out, and he cheerfully followed the Zoroastrian tenets of working hard, making money, enjoying the proceeds and giving generously.

"Look at this one," he said. He held a small plastic rectangle in his palm. "It's a Pac-Man."

"What's a Pac-Man?" Mariam said.

"It's on an Atari cartridge," Mukhtar said, ignoring the question. "I have an auction running in virtual as we speak with three bidders on Mars, two in the Venusian cloud-cities and one warlord on Ganymede all in the running."

"Where did you get it?" Mariam said, because Mukhtar loved talking about his business and how he got things and how much he sold those same things for and all the profits he'd made. He claimed not to care about the various objects he sold but he wasn't fooling anyone, least of all his clients. He was a terrible enthusiast for old, useless, rare things. They all were.

"I got it from some kid who was rooting inside an old Millennium Vault out in Oman. Amazing. The amount of garbage you find in these things—all kinds of digital ghosts and potpourri, and that's if the cores aren't all corrupted or if no one's robbed it by then. They're worse than the pyramids for robbing, those vaults. The people who made them always thought they were really clever in hiding them away, and that's what drives your average vault hunter, you know, the challenge. If you could find one. If you could find one that works. If you could find one that has something. Well, this kid had something and he didn't even know what he had. A Pac-Man! It's a part of history, it is. A valuable piece."

Mariam stared, because coming down the avenue towards them was a small and rather singular figure, pushing a cart in front of it, and it looked strangely familiar.

"I think we have a visitor," she said.

"Seller, or buyer?" Mukhtar said, still admiring his what-ever-it-was.

"I'd say seller, by the looks of him," Mariam said.

"Good, good. Let's make some tea, then."

"I don't think that would be necessary," Mariam said, still staring.

"What? Why not? I always make tea," Mukhtar said.

"Because it's a robot," Mariam said.

The doorbell rang. The shop checked the robot for weap-onry and started going haywire. The robot stood outside and waited politely.

Mariam pressed a button on an antique intercom and said, "All weaponry must be left outside."

The robot nodded. "I'm afraid I cannot do that," it said.

Mariam pressed the button again.

"Why not?" she said.

The robot nodded.

"I am the weaponry," it said.

"Is it a real one?" Mukhtar said. He brought up a virtual screen, scrolled through the diagnostics. "How fascinating. It's completely scrambled. How old are you? Wait." He nod-ded to Mariam, who pressed the button.

"How old are you?" she said.

The robot nodded.

"Old," it said.

"Let it in, let it in," Mukhtar said. "I will make tea. I always make tea."

Mariam pressed another button. The locks slid open. She pressed the first button again.

She said, "Come in."

The robot nodded. It pushed the door and came inside, wheeling its trolley. Then it stood there and looked at Mariam.

Mariam stared at the robot. It was patched and old and rusted, and recent sand had scoured its body down to the metal, and there were patches on him of what looked like dried blood.

"I know you," she said. "You were in the souk when I was selling flowers. A few days ago. I gave you a rose."

"And I thanked you," the robot said. It had voice like old sand grinding, and like smoke. It looked at her with what could have been curiosity.

"You get about," it said.

"I take what work I can."

The robot nodded. "It is nice to see you again," it said dubiously.

"You, too. I never asked your name."

"I seldom give it."

"My name is Mariam."

"Mariam," the robot said, with that same dubious tone. "Yes."

"What is that?" Mariam said. She pointed at the trolley. Laid out on the trolley were golden body parts. Legs, arms, a torso and a head.

"What does it look like?" the robot said.

"I am sure I don't know," Mariam said. "Can I offer you tea?"

"Tea?" said the robot. "Why would I want tea?"

"It's a custom," Mariam said. "It's polite."

The robot nodded. "Then yes," it said. "I shall have tea."

Mukhtar appeared then. He carried a tray with a tea set and some biscuits. He beamed at the robot.

"Welcome, welcome!" he said. "It is rare to see one of you old robots here in Neom."

"I get the sense Neom is quite happy without us," the robot said.

Mukhtar inched his head. "It may be so," he allowed. "They do not like old things here, much. Always with the new. They forget the new becomes the old, and that they will be just as old and obsolete in their turn."

"Yes," the robot said.

"Tea?" Mukhtar said. He laid the service down on a low table.

"Yes," the robot said. It sat down. Mukhtar sat down. The robot sipped the tea. It nibbled on a biscuit.

"Very nice," it said.

"Yes," Mukhtar said. He ate a biscuit and took a noisy sip of tea and cleared his throat. "Well, then. You are here to buy, or sell?"

The robot hesitated.

"Both, perhaps," it said. "Or neither."

Mukhtar indicated he was listening.

"You know what this is?" the robot said. It pointed to the relics on the trolley.

"Would you mind?" Mukhtar said. He got up to inspect them.

"Not at all," the robot said.

Mukhtar examined the objects. "A golden man," he said, almost whispering.

"Yes. You know it?"

"I thought it was a story," Mukhtar said. "I never saw one."

"There were not many made," the robot said. "Maybe there was only ever the one."

"What is it?" Mariam said. "What was it?"

"It's a robot," Mukhtar said.

"I can see that," Mariam said.

"Can it be fixed?" the robot said.

"Fixed? You think it is still *alive*?"

"You fix things, do you not, before you sell them?" the robot said. "It makes the value greater and so on. So I understand."

"I am just a dealer," Mukhtar said. "And this is. . . . Are you willing to *sell* it?" He withdrew from the golden man and paced.

"It would not be appropriate," Mukhtar said. "I do not deal in religious relics. It is not . . . proper."

"This is a religious relic?" Mariam said. By now she was confused.

"It is a weapon," the robot said. "But I do not think it is dangerous anymore. I do not know. It was made for an old war, and it is an old thing."

"I did hear there was a disturbance in the desert the other night," Mukhtar murmured. "A shurta patrol was attacked by wild machines."

"They should have kept away," the robot said. "It is not my fault."

"You dug it out?"

"Yes. It disturbed the local . . . wildlife. The old soldier machines out in the desert still. They remember. I do not rightly know if they were drawn to it to kill it or if they were called there by it. It doesn't seem alive to me. But some things are hard to kill."

"Zoroaster lived thousands of years ago, yet his faith still lives in me and my line," Mukhtar said. "The hardest thing to kill is truth."

"Yet as a weapon it failed," the robot said.

"I could make inquiries," Mukhtar said, a little unwillingly, Mariam thought. "But no one has made new robots for centuries. And this. . . . Some would say it is an abomination."

"It is just a machine," the robot said. "I would like it fixed."

"To sell?" Mukhtar said.

"No."

Mariam watched them. Mukhtar genuinely troubled, though Mariam did not quite understand why. And the robot, softly spoken, inflexible—she thought she could detect a burning desperation in its core, the way it stood. As though it had come a long way just for this.

And she thought of the Damask rose she had given it, and that it had carried into the desert beyond the city.

"Then can you pay for it yourself?" Mukhtar said. "What you are asking of me, it is expensive.'

"I do not have much money," the robot said.

"Then do you have anything else to sell?"

The robot considered the question.

"Would you value me?" it said.

"Value you?" Mukhtar said.

"Yes."

Mukhtar rose. "Would you mind . . . ?" he said.

"Not at all."

Mukhtar wasn't noded. He put on headgear, lenses with which to study the robot instead. He muttered as he went.

"You weren't kidding about the weaponry part," he said. "If you ever go off you'd blow half this city. You were never decommissioned?"

"I never felt the need," the robot said.

"You had the build upgraded on Titan," Mukhtar said.

"Yes."

"The left leg, it isn't an original. Though it is a good replica. Ceres?"

"You have a good eye," the robot said.

"Lost your leg in the war?"

"I lost a lot of things in the war," the robot said.

"You've had some augmentation, too," Mukhtar said. "I cannot make out the firmware at all. This is new occlusion protocols. Wildtech, at a guess. You went as far as Jettisoned?"

Mariam stared at the robot in fascination, for although Neom received visitors from across the inhabited worlds, she had never met anyone who had gone as far as Jettisoned, that lawless outpost on Charon. The people who went there seldom came back.

"My job got me about," the robot said. "And I did not mind the long journeys."

"Your job?" Mukhtar said sharply.

"I am a robot," the robot said. "I must make myself useful."

"Your skill set is somewhat restrictive," Mukhtar said.

"It is useful."

"You kill people?"

"A robot may not injure a human being or, through inaction, allow a human being to come to harm. . . . I try to follow the Way of Robot when I can. Of course, the Laws were only ever a philosophical concept, and I must live in the world as it is, not as we may wish it to be."

"That's a long-winded answer to a simple question."

The robot sighed. "Only when I get paid," it said. "So what do you think?"

"Of your value as object? You're missing some of the original parts. Your internal structure is hopelessly mangled with updates. And to be entirely honest with you, you're not in the greatest condition."

"I have noticed," the robot said.

"Not to mention it isn't strictly legal to deal in sentient-level machines," Mukhtar said. "Even in a place like Neom."

"Are we really sentient, though?" the robot said. "Or are we only very good at pretending?"

"That's a philosophical question," Mukhtar said. He shrugged. "To the right collector, sure. You'd be worth a fair bit. More if I strip you for parts. Is that what you want?"

"It is a conundrum," the robot said. "I do need my parts. I do not know."

"This . . . thing. Is it really that important to you?"

"It was once. Perhaps it still is."

Mukhtar nodded. "Would you care to leave it here, for

now? I will study it more carefully. There is someone I could ask. It might be possible to repair."

"I would like that," the robot said. "Thank you."

"Are you sure you won't sell it?" Mukhtar said, a little wistfully.

"I am sure," the robot said. It got up. "Thank you for your time, and your hospitality."

"You're very welcome."

The robot nodded to Mariam. "It was nice to see you again," it said.

"You, too."

"Goodbye."

The robot left. Mariam let out a breath of air she hadn't realised she was holding.

"Is it really a killer?" she said.

"Oh, yes," Mukhtar said.

"I thought robots were peaceful."

"They were made to do what people needed them to," Mukhtar said. "But there's a strong market in combat artefacts. It's why people still go out into the desert every year to try and hunt down UXOs. Even when it's dangerous. This thing, though. . . . A golden man. It isn't even supposed to exist."

Mariam looked at the heaped pile of metallic golden body parts the robot had left behind.

"I wonder what happened to it," she said.

8.
THE MECHANIC

MUKHTAR, MEANWHILE, wondered the same thing.

On the outskirts of the city, where the green belt of greenhouses met the unforgiving bitterness of desert, there lay a scattered asteroid belt of temporary homes and habitats, and it was there that he went with his query.

The woman he sought was busy outside, despite the heat. She wore blue overalls and the parts of vintage motorcycles and even diesel cars lay all about her, and Mukhtar was unpleasantly reminded of when the peninsula was known mostly for its oil. The toll the age of petrol had taken on the planet could still be felt in unpredictable storms and those parts of the world that were only now being re-terraformed. Mukhtar himself had a congenital respiratory disorder as a genetic remnant of that age; and he maintained it by regular injection of nano-vapour that pulsed repair machines into his lungs. He never let it stop him, and he didn't think of it very often. But these custom repair jobs were an unwelcome reminder all the same.

"Salam alaikum, Sharif," he said.

Sharif turned and saw him. She waved. "Wa alaikum salam, Mukhtar. Be with you in a minute."

"Take your time."

Mukhtar perched himself down on a rock and watched the mechanic at work. Sharif worked with the quiet confidence of experience. She picked objects that were incomprehensible to Mukhtar. She weighed them, considered, discarded, picked another, and somehow or another was assembling these relics into a single creation, bit by bit, until a slick and powerful machine stood in the sand.

"What is it?" Mukhtar said.

Sharif shrugged. "A bore-rider, I think," she said.

"You don't know?"

"I let the parts decide."

"Where do you get the parts?"

"From the zabaleen."

Sharif wiped her hands on a piece of cloth and came over. "Coffee?"

"Please."

She went to a table and began preparing the drink. She carried a tray over. Mukhtar accepted the coffee gratefully. They sat and sipped. Mukhtar wiped his forehead. It was very hot outside. Sharif saw but said nothing. Not far in the distance the great turbines turned and the sand filter walls shimmered.

"Speaking of parts," Mukhtar said. "I wanted to show you something."

"Of course."

Mukhtar brought out sheaves of paper. He did not like committing things to the great virtuality that was invisibly all around them. Not when it came to business. Instead he showed Sharif the blueprints he had drawn himself.

"You always bring me something curious . . ." Sharif said. She seemed engrossed in the blueprints. Mukhtar poured a second cup of coffee for them both.

"Are you asking hypothetically?" Sharif said at last. She raised her head and stared at him, and there was something discomfiting about her stare.

"No," Mukhtar told her.

"You have seen this? With your own eyes?"

"The parts are in my emporium."

Sharif shook her head.

"This is bad business," she said.

"How so?"

"For one, a golden man was not meant to exist."

"And yet it does," Mukhtar said.

Sharif studied the blueprints. "Unless it doesn't," she said.

"What do you mean?"

"Does it work?" Sharif said.

"No."

"It could be a fake," she told him.

"I thought of that," Mukhtar said. "But even fakes of this nature are valuable."

"Why did you bring it to me?"

"Who else will I bring this to, Sharif? Your authority is undisputed."

She stared at him some more.

". . . True," she allowed at last.

"I wonder," Mukhtar said, almost apologetically, "if you could make it work."

"Make it work?" She frowned. "I could put it together again, yes, if that is what you are asking. You ran a deep scan, of course?"

"Of course. But the results make no sense to me."

"It uses wildtech," she told him. "*Nakaimas*. If that's intact then it could work, if it were genuine. And you have the head, the arms, the legs. Most of the parts."

"Yes."

"Where did you find it?" she said.

"Some old robot dug it out in the desert somewhere."

"And do you trust it?" Sharif said.

"The robot? It does not seem the trustworthy sort," Mukhtar said. "An old assassin from the war, if I am any judge. But it seems genuine in its desire to recover the object."

"*Object* is not a word one should apply to something like this."

"Is it alive, then? Sentient?"

Sharif drank coffee. She took her time. She said, "What it truly is I don't know. It is just a story told sometimes, and then in quiet voices. A golden man. A weapon. Or perhaps a work of art. Do you remember New Punt? It was a freeport town between Mecca and Medina, after the age of oil and before the Exodus ships were built in Mars orbit. It was prosperous, a city of gold."

"Like old Punt."

"Yes. And like old Punt it is lost. It vanished off the records. Go there now and you will find nothing but desert where a city once was. Where people lived and died and traded. Not even ghosts remain."

Mukhtar wiped sweat and still felt chilled. Punt was a story. His grandfather told him tales of its riches. The city had grown so powerful it raised the enmity of powerful polises. A war broke out. Punt held strong, until a miracle visited the city in the night. And in the morning the city was gone as though it had never existed.

"The miracle?" he said.

"It could be. It might be."

"But it's just a story."

"True." Sharif shrugged. "It is most likely a fake," she said. "But a good one. Besides, there's no way to prove it one way or the other. It's worthless to you in its current condition."

"How so?" Mukhtar said.

"It has no beating heart," she told him.

"Its power source?"

She nodded. "It must have been taken out of it when it was broken apart and buried in the desert. It would suggest someone had the right idea to dispose of it safely. It's possible it isn't genuine but someone still went to the trouble of destroying it. I could rebuild it for you, good as new. But without the heart you'll have a simple golden mannequin and nothing more."

"I would like that," Mukhtar said. "If you could rebuild it. I will pay twice the usual rate."

"That is acceptable," Sharif said.

"What is the power source?" Mukhtar said. "It can't be hard to find a replacement, surely?"

Sharif shook her head. "They say it used a miniature black hole enclosed within a statis field." She smiled as though she'd told a foolish joke. "Can you get your hands on one?"

"A black hole for a heart?"

"That is the story."

"But that's ridiculous. The only people mad enough to play with exotic matter weapons were—"

But he didn't even want to say it.

"Terrorartists. Yes," Sharif said. "And they're just as much a story to frighten children with."

"There is a considerable market for terrorartist artefacts," Mukhtar said.

"You deal in such materiel?" she said sharply.

"Sometimes. Not often. Decommissioned work. They seldom come up on the market."

"They say you could never truly decommission them," Sharif said. "Besides, how does one make safe a work of mass murder?"

"They didn't only kill," Mukhtar said. "'Mad' Rucker seeded the Boppers on Titan, and they're harmless lifeforms."

"Only as far as you know," Sharif said. "Who can tell what their ultimate purpose is? The terrorartists seeded destruction like gardeners planting trees. They thought long-term. When you plant an olive tree you don't do it for yourself but for your descendants. They did the same with death."

The day was hot and the coffee was finished. Mukhtar was uneasy with the conversation. He heard Sharif. But in his heart he longed to see the golden man and what it did. For terror and awe went together, and people still came to gawk at Sandoval's *Earthrise*, or the time-frozen destruction of Rohini's Jakarta bomb on Java.

"*Who* made it?" he asked then.

"Excuse me?"

"The golden man. Was it attributed to any . . . *artist* in particular?"

He didn't like calling them *artists*. Making mass death and destruction into art seemed to Mukhtar to be serving falsehood; a contamination of both the living and the dead. An artist, it seemed to Mukhtar, should follow truth. The terrorartists sowed chaos. Their art was an act of polluting the world.

And yet he could not deny the terrible beauty in their work.

"She called herself Nasu," Sharif said.

9.
THE SYBIL

WHEN THE GREEN CARAVANSERAI arrived in the town of El Quesir it was late afternoon. The sun dipped low in the sky and the boats on the Red Sea cast long jagged reflections over the water.

Elephants trumpeted; goats bleated; children ran laughing at the sight of the ocean.

The great khans of the caravan reconfigured and settled themselves beyond the city's demarcation line. Saleh and Elias climbed down and stood on the dusty earth.

"I want to go into the town," Saleh said.

"We are not supposed to go into the town," Elias said.

Saleh shrugged. "Then don't come," he said.

Elias looked hurt.

"It is an old place," he said. "An old city. The pharaohs held it and it was old even then. The old expeditions to Punt went out from here."

"What was Punt?" Saleh said.

"A kingdom of gold," Elias said. "But it is lost now."

Saleh thought of lost things. He thought of his father, still dying in that temporal bomb in Dahab.

Forever dying. Forever out of reach.

But he had cried his tears. He kept trying to tell himself that.

He wanted to sell his one thing of value and be done with it all. Start new.

Be new.

Elias, reading his expression, said, "El Quesir is not a good place to find a buyer."

"Why not?"

"It is a buyer's place on the way to other destinations." Elias hesitated. "They sell black-market things here, too."

"All the more reason to go," Saleh said. "Are you coming, or what?"

"I can't let you go on your own," Elias said, "they'll eat you up in El Quesir. So, yes."

"I've been to a city before," Saleh said.

"I'm sure you have," Elias said kindly.

The two boys crossed the road. It wasn't long before the city swallowed them. The narrow alleyways twisted and turned. Washing hung on lines overhead. A cat yawned in a doorway. They stopped at a falafel stand and had a half each, then wandered down to the beach and Saleh saw the sea.

The sun was low in the sky. Slow airships glided over the water, travelling from Cairo to Mecca or back from Djibouti to Aqaba or Eilat. Three floating islands hovered in the distance. Beyond the sea, on the distant shore, he thought he could just make out the outline of mountains and a glittering sprawl of lights along the coast.

"What's there?" he said, pointing.

"That's Neom," Elias said, and the sudden name filled Saleh with a longing he could not articulate.

They wandered along the beach. El Quesir felt strangely deserted at that hour, perhaps always. Dusk settled and the mosques called the faithful to prayer, and the sound had a scratchy, echoey quality to it. They went past the port and here the streets grew busier, and neon lights lit doorways set into old stone walls, where food cooked on open coals and smoke poured out of metal braziers.

Familiar Arabic mingled here with Chinese and Asteroid Malay, some Russian. The figures sitting in the street were hooded in shadows. They drank coffee and spoke in low voices. Saleh and Elias went deeper into the alleys until the space opened into one large open-air market. Elias was hailed a few times and he acknowledged politely: the Green Caravanserai were known and familiar here.

Saleh felt lost again, out of his depth. This was not like the Ghost Coast. A bar with an aquatic theme held an aquarium of tentacle junkies who pressed their faces to the glass and stared out at him, their suckered arms beating rhythmically to underwater music.

"You want Drift Tar?" someone said, materialising out of the shadows. He was small and stooped.

"We don't want Tar," Elias said politely.

They passed tables covered in old guns. Elderly men sat on low chairs watching camel racing on an ancient screen. The whole place felt old, semi-abandoned. El Quesir seemed to Saleh like a sunken ship crusted in salt, still tilting impossibly half out of the water. In the next street they sold bio-relics: this Saleh knew better. He stopped at the exhibits, recognising Leviathan blubber, hardened in death into an amber-like substance. It was near impossible to cut. Then he saw roc's eggs, two of them. He looked more closely.

"This one's a fake," he said. He nearly smiled. The Abu-Ala were not above passing forgeries when they were low on the real thing. Stealing a roc's egg was dangerous work. But making a good fake was art.

"Who asked you?" the seller said.

Elias took Saleh's arm and pulled him away before he got into a fight.

They bought kofta off a grill and ate it hot with their fingers. They came to a place of fortune tellers then. An ancient robotnik sat begging in a corner. His bowl was filled with bits of machinery. He looked up at Saleh, then looked away.

"You know that you don't *have* to stay with us," Elias said.

Saleh felt ashamed, because Elias was his friend.

"The caravan life isn't for everyone," Elias said. "It isn't for most people. You don't have to stay with us till Bahrain. Nothing is keeping you with us—nothing."

Elias looked down when he said it. He didn't meet Saleh's eyes.

"I'm so sorry, Elias," Saleh said. "I don't know what I want."

"You are still grieving."

Saleh took the other boy's hand in his.

"All I know is where I don't belong," he said miserably. "And there is nowhere that I do belong."

"I was born into the caravan," Elias said. "But I remain by choice. It is my home. My life. It's family."

Saleh nodded. It was decided then between them, silently, he realised.

He would not return to the caravan with Elias.

"I will miss you," Saleh said.

"I will miss you too," Elias said.

As they stood in an embrace a woman watched them from a doorway. Her face was hidden in a cowl. Above her head was a neon sign that said, simply, *Fortune Teller*.

"You wish to see your future?" the fortune teller said. Saleh and Elias drew apart. Saleh stared at the woman suspiciously.

"I know my future," Elias said.

"No one knows their future," the fortune teller said.

"So then what do you practice?" Elias said. "No offence."

"None taken, Elias," the woman said.

Saleh smiled. He knew those tricks, his aunt read fortunes too.

"You heard us speaking," he said.

"I never said I didn't. Come. The future is uncertain but by looking at the past one can discern the eddies and currents of probabilities. All I ask for payment is that which you are willing to freely give."

"And what is that?" Elias said.

A jackal watched them from the shadows. Saleh saw its

bright eyes. The jackal grinned at him and shook its head as though in warning. The fortune teller ignored Elias's question. She went inside. Saleh hesitated, but he was curious, and what harm could it do? He went in after her and Elias followed.

The room was dark, the ceiling low. Incense burned, too sweetly. The room was oddly furnished. Saleh saw rough wooden tables, long and heaped with parts. He saw a robot's head, a gene sequencer, a cracked roc's egg, an artificial womb and incubator, screwdrivers and blowtorches and a small black monolith that made his head hurt when he stared at it. The room looked like a workshop.

The smell of the incense made him sleepy and he found it hard to focus his gaze. The fortune teller led them to a table and a metal bowl filled with viscous liquid.

Saleh held Elias's hand as he stared into the bowl. The fortune teller began to stir the liquid with her finger.

Patterns formed.

"They distill this substance only on Jettisoned," the fortune teller said. Her voice was low, melodious. "Just an ounce of Probability Water shipped across space from the Outer System will make a pauper out of a prince." She laughed, low and throaty. Saleh stared at the patterns that formed.

"Each drop of water is packed with quantum processors," the fortune teller said. "The reflection it sends shows you your future . . . futures . . . likelihoods and chances, destiny and fate. Your eyes are growing heavy. You are feeling very relaxed. Follow the sound of my voice. . . . I will count down now and you will sleep, three, two, one."

Saleh smiled. Is that all it was? he thought. An old Mesmer

routine, nothing else. He felt content, in charge of his faculties. Just a shiny prop and old-fashioned hypnotism. He felt perfectly at ease, without the need to do anything but stand there.

"Good, good," the fortune teller said distractedly. She stirred the liquid and images burst into Saleh's eyes. He was a bopper, hopping and slithering on the surface of Titan under the purple roiling skies; then he floated in space, with Jupiter rising, a mine taking part in the Trifala King War, watching as odd craft cruised past him; then he was farther still, a comet blazing past the strange inhabited moons of Oberon and Titania; then farther, always farther, until the sun was a tiny ball of cold light hanging in space, and in the black of the Oort he thought he saw something impossible: enormous entities the size of worlds, with tendrils of black matter pulsing and reaching far into space, and he felt their attention turn on him, and tried to flee, and was lost. . . .

"Well that's done with," the fortune teller said. "And you can't say I wasn't fair, I always carry a job through." She moved away from the table and removed her hood. Saleh, in his trance-like state, half-saw the dark entities and half the fortune teller, but though she had removed her hood her face was still somehow hidden from him.

"Don't worry," she said, as though reading his mind, "you won't remember this." She reached for his bag and rummaged through it, and Saleh didn't stop her, even when she extracted his one possession of value out of it. The fortune teller stared at it in interest.

"Dahab," she said. "I forgot all about that one."

Saleh wanted to tell her about the explosion, about his father still caught in that slow bubble of time; about how he felt both felled and free; how guilt and relief mixed inside him. He wanted to tell her about the stars and where he wanted to go and what he wanted to do.

"Hush," the fortune teller said. "You think so loudly and it's all jumbled up. Everyone feels guilty for something. And everyone wants to be free. I'd say, don't be so trite, only you're young. You'll either grow up to accept it or it will eat you inside—I'll bet on the second, it's what people usually end up doing. Now, what is this?" She shook the canister of the old time-dilation bomb. "It's empty, the poor thing. That was a hack job, you know, back in Dahab, just a copy-cat of Rohini's better work. But all artists begin by imitating others. It is nothing to be ashamed of." She put the canister to her ear and listened to it.

"Yes, yes, the poor thing," she said. "It needs to sing again."

She took it with her to another side of the room and started going through stuff on the tables like a shopper in a bazaar.

"Where did I put it?" she said. "You know, Saleh, back in— well, whenever it was, it was a long time ago—I went to the Up and Out too, I had had enough of Earth and also, to be truthful, I was what you'd call a fugitive, and I needed to fake my death and vanish for a while—a few centuries, at least, or that was what I figured then. The old gang is mostly gone now. 'Mad' Rucker, who wasn't really mad, and Rohini and the others. One of them made the Silentude out in the Oort. I think. I went as far as Jettisoned and I learned all kinds of things but then I came back. The world is much the same as when I'd left it. A little too peaceful for my liking, maybe. But we can change that. The past is all around us, as you well know. And it is far too easy to call it back to life. Ah, here. Listen. How beautifully it sings!"

She held something in her hands. Saleh couldn't make out what it was. The fortune teller did something to the bomb canister. She put it to her ear again.

"It hums," she said. She put it back in Saleh's bag.

"It will be more valuable now," she told him. "Much more valuable. You'll see.

Saleh blinked and found himself standing alone in a small stone courtyard. It was dawn. He stared around him in confusion. A faded sign above a doorway said *Fortune Teller*, but the entrance was littered with junk and it was clear no one had used the place for years.

What was he doing there? He remembered the caravan, and deciding to go. He remembered holding Elias.

Then a conviction: he had decided already he wasn't going back to the Green Caravanserai.

He lifted his bag. It felt heavier somehow. A jackal watched Saleh from the courtyard's archway.

"I tried to . . . warn you," it said.

"Warn me about what?" Saleh said distractedly. Then, "You're Anubis."

"You . . . remember."

"What are you doing here?" Saleh said.

"I grew tired with . . . the desert," Anubis said.

"Yeah," Saleh said with feeling. "Me too."

He started to walk, and Anubis trotted beside him. They went through the narrow alleyways of El Quesir and came to the port, where gulls cried and the sea spray rose over the breakers in the clear early morning air. The horizon shimmered.

"Where to, then?" Anubis said.

Saleh stared across the water.

"Neom," he said quietly.

10.
THE JACKAL

A NUBIS COULD SCENT THE GHOSTS and the fragments of souls in the air all throughout El Quesir. He trotted alongside Saleh. The Bedouin boy was a strange one, he had ghosts all over him and didn't even know it. Jackals were good at smelling revenants. Back in the war they were used as trackers for the dead, sniffing out soldiers who could still be repurposed.

Anubis remembered with scent-memory passed to him by his ancestors: going through sand and storms, pulling out corpses half-buried, ripping out the soul-catchers in the bases of their skulls. Digital memory intertwined with gooey biological matter. The human brain stopped at death but the data in the node lingered. It gave out a smell all its own.

"How get . . . Neom?" he asked Saleh.

The boy chewed on an apple.

"Ship," he said.

"Anubis don't like . . . sea."

Anubis didn't like a lot of things. A small vocabulary and an insufficient speaking apparatus that did not allow him to express himself properly with humans. They lacked the elegance of jackal speech. He did better communicating with the Others in the Conversation, but the digitals seldom paid attention to the brief lives of biological creatures, and when they spoke, the high-density screech of their voices made his ears bleed.

"It's not a long crossing," Saleh said, not unkindly. "It's only a narrow sea."

Anubis was noded but the desert didn't offer much feed. Here in the city it was denser, richer. He'd decided a while back that he was bored with the Sinai, and certainly with the company of the Webster, who was as mad as any of that clan, and besides he had a feeling a jackal with his particular skill set might make his fortune out in the world.

While jackals had been augmented and given speech and ghost-scent for the war, it was so long ago that barely anyone remembered. Anubis only knew it from the smell-stories. He used his skills to hunt for old forgotten ghosts out in the desert. What remained of people after centuries were bones and a small hard disc, and he collected the discs and the Webster traded them sometimes for other goods.

Long ago, Anubis became curious about the site of the downed spaceship that fell not far from the Webster house. He'd gone sniffing around there, pulled by the tales of treasure, but like others before him he found nothing. Someone had cleaned the site up long ago. Whatever treasure the *Compassionate Heaven* carried, it was long gone, if it ever was to begin with.

He saw the two boys go there, too. Had followed them. Anubis did not fancy joining the caravan. He didn't like the elephants, or the goats, or children. But he thought it might be good to follow at a distance for a while. After Saleh and Elias came back from the ship, and the moon rose in the sky, Anubis went back to the site of the crash for one last sniff, just on a whim.

This time, though, the site *did* smell different. Some old, not unfamiliar traces first: scavengers, the Webster. Then, just recently, the two boys. But in between was a new smell, sharp and half in the digitality: star anise and pixelated Byzantine Blue and rust.

It made Anubis scared.

It made Anubis *hungry*.

He followed the trace. He couldn't help it. The smell exerted a power over him, both biological and augmented brain. It wasn't something he knew, it was something he *felt*.

He trotted after it all night, losing it at times but always picking it up again, until he came to a cave high in the mountains where clouds black with rain watered a poisoned earth.

Anubis entered the cave. The smell he sought was stronger here, rancid and rank. The person who left it was only recently departed from that place.

Anubis found human furniture, a bed and a desk. He found remnants of food on the table, and two glasses, both empty and both smelling of an old, expensive liqueur. Ganymedian brandy, if Anubis was any judge. It was near priceless.

He looked, but he couldn't find the bottle.

What he *did* find was a human skeleton. The bones were

old and there was no flesh left. The brain was long gone, but the nodal stem had been left, and Anubis could pick just a spark of life in the quantum processors. He clamped his jaws on the spine and the old bones snapped easily, and he removed the ghost of the human, but when he pulled it out the last flecks of life faded away from it, and Anubis thought he could sense tired relief from the ghost before it was gone. Anubis let the disc drop to the floor and then he sniffed around some more.

He wondered who the two drinkers had been, and where they had gone. It was possible one was the skeleton, he supposed, though that made very little sense. But the whole place was weird and made very little sense. Something kept bothering him, as though eyes were staring at him in the dark, but he could smell no one there. Finally he came to a small wooden chest and opened it, again with his teeth, and for a moment he thought it was empty.

Then he saw that at the bottom, its grey colour camouflaging it against the dark of the box, was a small rough-hewn chunk of rock. He tried to reach it, though the digital smell repulsed him. When he finally managed to close his teeth on it he almost retched. This, too, was alive in some way, but it wasn't human. When he tuned in directly to the Conversation, the rock manifested as a block of solid code, impenetrable and foreign. Whatever it was, it wasn't currently active, but it was conscious: Anubis could smell that.

A part of him wanted to throw this revenant away. Another part was curious, and curiosity got the better of him. He didn't have hands but he did have a special pouch tied to his body and he put the rock in there.

He went back to the caravan though he didn't stay too close. He still didn't like the elephants.

Then he smelled the sea again, one day, and he saw the two boys slink out into the old town and he followed them.

Anubis had never been to El Quesir before, had never, in truth, left the desert proper, and so he was delighted with the strange alleyways and the enchanting smells of laundry overhead and falafel and manure, spice from the many shops, the sea and coal smoke and the smell of people. He happily chewed on a dead bird he'd found by some bins. City life suited him so far, he thought.

It was easy to follow Elias and Saleh. But when he found them again Anubis retreated into the shadows. They stood by an abandoned yard with a faded sign over it, and seemed to be speaking to thin air. The smell, however, was familiar, and strong: the same smell from the downed ship, the same as inside the cave.

"I wouldn't go . . . in there," he growled. But the boys didn't hear him or, if they did, they paid no attention.

Anubis watched them go in. He fell asleep, and when he woke he felt a hand brush through his fur and he shivered, for there was no one there, and a voice in his mind said, mockingly, *Nice doggy*.

Then it was gone, the smell and the voice. When Saleh came out alone, Anubis said, "I tried to . . . warn you."

———————

They walked together to the harbour. The sun was very bright and the gulls cried in the distance, and Anubis smelled the sea and thought of distant shores.

"Where to, then?" he said.

The boy stared across the water.

He said, "Neom."

So they got on a ship and went there.

11.
THE SHELTER

THE ROBOT PASSED THE INTERSECTION of Ansari and Khayyam and came to the Square of Future Prosperity, where pigeons congregated around the large Statue of the Unknown Scientist. The robot bought a packet of sunflower seeds from a woman who sold them from a kiosk, and it opened the packet and scattered the seeds on the grass and the pigeons came and pecked at the robot's feet.

Nannies went past pushing their charges. Small children played in a sand pit. An elderly couple, clearly tourists from some other, less youthful place, came and sat on a bench and watched the children play. Sprinklers whoosh-whooshed water over the manicured grass. The robot stood perfectly still. The sun was high in the sky but a cool breeze blew through that small city square from hidden air conditioners.

"Hey, mister," a small child said. The robot turned and looked down at the little human.

"Yes?" it said.

"Are you a spaceman?"

The robot gave it some consideration.

"I am not a man," it said. "But I have been to space."

"What's it like, mister?"

"Space?" the robot said. "It smells like hot metal and grilled lamb and sulfur. Both sweet and metallic. Or so I'm told. I cannot smell."

"You're funny," the child said. Then she waddled away.

The robot crumpled the empty packet of seeds in its hand and put it into a waste bin provided. Then it left the square. It followed the exit signs and made its way farther along the road until the shiny new buildings gave way to the older structures of the Nineveh Quarter, and people's clothes took on a secondhand quality. Butchers sold diced mutton and goat, a four-armed preacher standing on a produce box entreated the passersby to seek salvation in the zero-point field.

"You, sir!" the preacher said, pointing at the robot. "Step right up and find redemption! Let God's true love shield you from the Nine Billion Hells! Have you heard the word of Dr. Novum, who came back from the stars? I have some literature I would love to share with you if you would just—"

"I am not a sir," the robot said, a little reproachfully.

"Excuse me?" the preacher said.

"Can you point me in the general direction of the ersatz shelter?" the robot said.

"Ersatz? Down the road, past the Lebanese bakery and the Lottery stand, then left on Yokoi. You'll start to see them. Or not, I suppose. But are you sure you wouldn't like to hear of the gospel of Dr. Novum, who came back from the stars and—"

"Yes, yes," the robot said. "The stars." It left the preacher where he stood and walked down the road, past the Lebanese bakery and a stand for the Yiwu Lottery. The robot bought a ticket from the seller at the stand, because although winners were rare, the Lottery, it was said, was everywhere—and it always granted one's true heart's desire.

The robot didn't have a heart, of course, but a game of chance was a game of chance and there were things it wanted—desired, even. It stopped on the corner of Yokoi and bought a cheap pair of goggles, and put them awkwardly over its head.

"Aren't you noded?" the young woman who sold the robot the goggles said.

"Mind your own business," the robot said. "Begging your pardon."

"You look stupid in them," the young woman said.

The robot supposed it *could* have noded itself, at the very least attached an aug to its own ancient systems, so that it could see and participate in the Conversation, that virtuality of worlds that was all around it, as persistent as air and, to its users, as essential. But the robot was old and in a business that valued privacy; in a world that was always connected there was enormous value in being unplugged.

In the old days of the war the robot had run sneakersnets to carry information, data stored on isolated devices and carried physically from place to place. The same old networks were still active throughout the solar system, as the robot well knew. And data couriers amputated from the Conversation could earn a living ferrying hardcoded information on slow, anonymous runs.

Now the robot stared out at the street through the knock-off goggles. A dragon-like creature curled in a doorway, pink and bright orange in colour. It blinked sleepily at the robot and blew out fire. An ekans and a raichu played together under a leaking tap. A sad Gojira towered over the street. It leaned down abruptly and swallowed a Zommer just under the robot's feet. The robot went on as the street filled with creatures it could only see through the goggles. A Namco Pac-Man chased a ghost. A furby waddled after a speeding hedgehog.

The robot came to a gate with a sign that said, *Sims Shelter, if no answer use side door.*

The robot rang the bell. A tamagotchi chattered at it excitedly. The robot raised its foot and the tamagotchi shrieked and vanished behind the feet of the woman who came out of the shelter.

The robot stared at Mariam.

"Come *on*," it said.

"You are here to adopt a pet?" Mariam said. She stared at the robot distrustfully. "You don't strike me as the pet-keeping type."

"A bit rude," the robot said. "Do you work here, too?"

"I fill in sometimes," Mariam said. "I'm just a volunteer."

"Of course you are," the robot said.

"So what *do* you want?" Mariam said.

"Can you let me in?"

"I suppose. Why are you wearing goggles?"

"To see them," the robot said.

"The poor things," Mariam said. She wore goggles too, though hers were more discreet and very slightly fashionable. "They brought the last wild pikachu here a few years back, still running off a decrepit bootleg server in some fallout shelter in Iceland. Oh, come on, then, I suppose. There's no harm."

The shelter was in a dilapidated stone building with the roof missing and its rooms and courtyard open to the sky. Without the goggles it was quiet. With them it teemed with virtual life.

A long, long time even before the robot came into existence, an artist named Karl Sims began to breed virtual lifeforms in his servers and, a few years later, others began to print the creatures thus evolved into soft robots. Here in the Sims Shelter all manner of strange, old, simple creatures hopped and hovered and gurgled and giggled and jabbered to themselves, salvaged from who knew were, hosted and kept secure.

Mariam watched the robot uneasily as it walked slowly among them, shunning the attentions of a centuries-old tamagotchi, ignoring a sleeping snorlax and a pack of tiny furbies.

What did it want? Mariam wondered. What was it looking for?

The robot went deeper into the maze of open corridors. It came to the large back yard. It scanned the virtual horizon.

Catz and dogz stared at the robot with curiosity. A Skull-Greymon skulked. The robot ignored them and went to the edge of the yard, where in the physicality there was only a patch of dry earth, a small half-wilted plant, and broken slabs of paving stones.

The robot knelt down with some difficulty. It reached for the plant that stuck out from between the stones. The robot's hand closed over the stem and Mariam watched, horrified, as the stem burst open in the robot's hand.

Particles hovered around the robot's fingers. They pixelated. But that couldn't be right. The flower was real.

Wasn't it?

Mariam could only watch as the thing opened and glowed; until a small bright shard of light rested in the robot's open palm. Mariam could see it without the goggles now.

Somehow, a piece of virtuality had hidden itself in the physical. There had been no plant.

And how did the robot even know this?

"Hello, old friend," the robot said.

The thing in the robot's hand pulsed. It was a little fuzzy ball with two large, guileless eyes. It blinked adorably. A line for a mouth, that curved up in a hopeful smile. Eight-bit animation, like a game asset from the dawn of the Conversation.

Kawaii as a defensive mechanism: and whatever this thing was, it was old.

The line of a mouth moved. "I thought you were dead," it said.

"No," the robot said. And, "I am back."

The eyes blinked, cutely. The mouth moved.

"Why?" the thing in the robot's palm said.

"You know why."

The thing's mouth made a moue and sighed. It was so cute, Mariam thought.

"You were always sentimental," the thing said. "You should know better than to dig up the past."

"You won't help me?"

The thing sighed again. "Do I have a choice?"

"I could leave you here again, to hide out the centuries. But that is no more your nature than it is mine."

"But it *is* my nature," the thing said. "Lie low, blend in, survive. And it has been restful. Besides, I am only a sliver. The rest of me is gone."

"What *is* that?" Mariam said. The thing blinked in surprise. The robot turned its head and regarded her gravely.

"It is a soul," the robot said.

"A sliver of a soul," the soul corrected him. "I am dead, not even a ghost, really." It looked quite pleased with itself, somehow.

"Whose soul?" Mariam said. A terrible thought struck her. "The golden man?"

"You *did* go digging!" the soul said accusingly. "Don't you ever learn? *She* will hear of it, I can guarantee it. *She* will come."

"She is long gone into the Up and Out," the robot said.

"Fool!" the soul said. "Put me back."

"It is a bit late for that, isn't it?" the robot said.

The thing blinked miserably. "I wish you didn't come," it said.

"I made a promise," the robot said.

"Fool," the soul said again. Then it fell quiet.

The robot closed its hand over the soul. It lifted it gently, then opened its mouth and swallowed. The soul vanished with a soft effect of pixelated diffusion.

The robot turned to Mariam.

"Thank you," it said.

"For what?" Mariam said.

"For helping me, when you don't have to," the robot said. "For being kind. I am not used to kindness."

Mariam was touched, but didn't know how to show it. She just nodded.

The robot nodded back. It turned to leave, and Mariam thought that she still had no understanding of it, of what it wanted, what it wished; what drove it.

But perhaps it didn't matter. Small kindnesses, not large: like a freely given flower.

"Wait," she said, on impulse. But the robot was already gone.

12.
THE SHAKE

NASIR WAS SITTING facing the door when he saw the robot come in.

The robot stood framed in the harsh sunlight from outside and its face was in shadow. Nasir sipped noisily on his milkshake. He had liked them since he was a little boy.

The robot approached, and Nasir sighed. He liked to come to Bashir's Shakes at that hour of the day, after a shift, when it was quiet. He always took a booth. He did not like being disturbed.

"You do not like me much, do you?" the robot said. It remained standing and waited our Nasir.

"Why are you here?" Nasir said, seeing that the robot wouldn't go away.

"Here, in Neom?" the robot said. "Here, on Earth? Here, as in existing? Why do any of us exist?"

"*Here*," Nasir said. "Why would you come here unless you drank milkshakes."

"Oh," the robot said. "I see. You are right. I do not usually consume mammary secretions. I can, of course, if I choose. It can still be turned into energy to power me. That is one way we robots were built. We can eat anything, if *eat* is the right word. But what is eating if not converting matter into energy? Humans do it, and so we do it. Yes, I will have a milkshake. Is there any flavour you would recommend?"

Nasir sighed again. "I like strawberry," he said.

"Very well," the robot said. "I will have that, too." It signalled to Bashir, who hurried over.

"One strawberry shake of your finest, please," the robot said. Bashir looked to Nasir, who nodded, and the proprietor withdrew.

"He seeks your approval," the robot observed. "Would you mind if I sat?"

"He worries," Nasir said, "about having a strange robot known for killing people come wandering into his house. And I do mind if you sit, but I don't suppose that will stop you so, please, do what you want."

"Thank you."

The robot pulled out a chair and sat opposite Nasir. It looked around.

"It is pleasant here," it said.

"It's quiet," Nasir muttered. "Usually."

"Again, I will observe you do not appear to care much for my presence."

"Yet here you are!" Nasir said, with more force than he'd perhaps intended. "Again. What do you *want*, robot? I don't even know your name."

"I am just a robot," the robot said. "You do not give names to your taps, or vehicles, or your toasters. Why must I have a name?"

"And yet you have one."

"I had one, once, it is true," the robot admitted. "There's no one alive to remember it, I would not think."

Bashir brought the milkshake and withdrew. The robot took a sip.

"Yes," it said dubiously. "It is rich in nutrients and sugar."

Nasir sat back. He'd lost his taste for strawberry. He said, "You followed me here?"

"Hardly *followed*." The robot set down the glass. "I asked around. I was told you often come here."

"That I do. But it doesn't explain what you want."

The robot considered. "I like Mariam," it said.

"I did not know robots can like."

"Can a robot love?" the robot said. "Can a robot hate? It is always dangerous to ascribe human emotions or motivations to machines."

"My point exactly," Nasir said.

"But I do like her," the robot said. "As confounding as she is. And I think you like her, too, do you not, Nasir?"

Nasir near blushed, which was embarrassing enough.

"What if I do?" he said.

"It is nothing to me, one way or the other," the robot said. "I am just making an observation I think to be true."

"We grew up together," Nasir said. "We were close as kids."

"You are not married?" the robot said.

"No."

"Why not?"

The robot seemed genuinely curious.

"I don't know. It never felt right."

"You struggle to form close relationships," the robot said.

"What are you?" Nasir said. "A counsellor?"

"I am equipped with human behaviour analysis modules," the robot said. "It was deemed a part of our basic battle tool-kit. Might be out of date now, though. Has human nature changed significantly in the past few centuries?'

"Not that I know," Nasir said. He stared across the table, interested despite himself. "What *are* you doing here, then?" he said.

"Here, in this shop? Talking to you. Drinking a milkshake. I have never had a milkshake before."

"Here, in Neom," Nasir said.

"You know what I am doing here."

"I know what you are *doing*," Nasir said. "I don't know why, or what you plan to do next. You showed up, dug a relic out in the desert and got all the UXOs agitated over it, had one of my people hurt, and now you're working as a hunter in the Game while trying to raise funds to fix whatever it is you dragged into my town from out in the desert. Is that about right?"

"I would allow that is a fair summation, yes," the robot said.

"Why? What is that thing? Why is it so important?"

"Who said it was important?" the robot said.

"It is important to you," Nasir said.

The robot was quiet.

"You assume I want to tell you my story," it said at last.

"Everyone always wants to tell their story," Nasir said. "The trick is finding someone who would listen."

The robot sipped its milkshake. It tipped its head. Nasir thought maybe it was imitating a human having a brain freeze. It said nothing.

"I worry," Nasir said, "that whatever it is you are doing will have ramifications for my city. We have few laws in Neom, but we do have order."

"Order," the robot said. Maybe scoffing. "In your pirate utopia. I visited Nirrti the Black on Titan, you know. There was less order, but more honesty there."

"I don't know anything about Titan," Nasir said. "But I know trouble when I see it walking into town."

"As you said, I am breaking no laws," the robot said. "Seeing as you have so few. What does a policeman *do* in this kind of town? Give out tickets for littering?"

"That's a part of it, yes," Nasir said.

"You may be right," the robot said. "I do bring disorder. Not by design—not mine, at any rate. I *was* designed."

"You say you cannot change your nature? That you were made only to destroy?"

"I was," the robot said.

"But you do think, you are *aware*, you speak—"

"Hath not a robot eyes? Hath not a robot hands?" the robot said. "Fed with the same food, hurt with the same weapons? If you poison us, do we not die? You think of Shylock, Nasir. But people always forget the point of Shylock's speech. If you wrong us, shall we not revenge? he asks. Shylock understood violence, and fighting back. If we are like you in the rest, we will resemble you in that."

"Then who hurt you?" Nasir said. "Were you wounded so badly that you seek revenge from centuries away? No one remembers the old wars."

"*I* remember," the robot said, and Nasir leaned back from the assault of its intent.

"Then let me help you. Let me stop it. Before it hurts my city."

"*Your* city!" the robot said. "You are like me. Made to serve. What is a policeman but a keeper of order on behalf of those who do the ordering? Always there are those who make the rules and those who enforce them."

"I sense you argue that I am like you," Nasir said.

"I *do* argue that you are like me," the robot said.

"Made to serve, and acting by one's nature."

"One's programming," the robot said.

"I feel like you have been telling yourself this for a long time," Nasir said. "In the hope that repetition will substitute for truth. You're smarter than that. Just because you can kill doesn't mean you should, or even want to. The war is over. Yet here you are, playing the part of the soldier still fighting on, trapped in a role of your choosing. Your war is over. You could be anything."

"Yet I will always be a robot," the robot said.

Nasir sighed. "I am a policeman because it's a job," he said, "yes. I must still work and, yes, in Neom the rich throw the trash and the poor pick it. I hear it's different on Mars, though not so different on Ganymede and Io. There are always systems of the world. All we can do is move through them. But we still get to choose how to be. *Who* to be."

"I feel like you have been telling yourself this for a long time," the robot said, "in the hope that repetition will substitute for truth.'"

Nasir smiled. His milkshake was finished. He said, "Neom is not an easy town. Not a fair one, either. But it is still my home. Mariam and I grew up here, we don't know another place. I can smell a scent and know exactly where I am. I can feel the ground change under my feet and walk on blindly. I can pass a corner and remember when I was a boy and walking past it with my mother. These things matter. It is home."

"Home," the robot said dubiously; as though it had never heard the word before.

"Yes," Nasir said.

"It must be nice, believing in one," the robot said. "But I have lived too long. That corner that you passed? I saw it when it was desert. A wall was built. A boy walked with his mother. The winds blew as they would. The mother died, the boy grew up. He kept the order, for a while. Then he too vanished. In time there will be sand again, and nothing else. All memory forgotten. Nothing to say the boy had ever lived, or died, or walked the earth.'

"That's nihilistic," Nasir said. "And if you think like that then your business of revenge is futile, too, for it will come to pass and be forgotten, so why bother? I am alive *now*. This is home *now*. What I do now is what matters. Leave my city alone. Do not bring chaos that you can't control. I will not tell you again."

"We seem doomed to disagree on certain matters," the robot said. "Very well. I will bear in mind your warning."

The robot stared at the empty glasses on the table.

"Milkshake," it said dubiously. "I do not think I care for it.'

"Maybe try chocolate next time," Nasir said.

13.
THE ROBOT

THEY STUDIED EACH OTHER across the table.

Nasir could sense the robot wanted—needed—to talk.

"So?" he said.

The robot nodded, as though it had reached a decision at last.

"I will not tell you about the war," the robot said. "But I will tell you what happened after."

"If you want," Nasir said.

He settled back to listen. He was good at listening, he knew that much.

"The war ended and we were left destitute," the robot said. "Many of the UXOs hid in the desert and are there to this day. But what were the anthropomorphous robots to do? We were not designed to hide and skulk. We were designed for people. Only the people forgot us.

"I say designed but in that I mean only the overall shape of our physicality. By the time I was made, the factories were themselves robots. Fully autonomous, and no human had set foot in them for years. Nor were we all alike. Like the Others, our consciousness was evolved in the digital breeding grounds. Each one of us formed through billions of evolutionary cycles of code competing with code. Each of us was different, just like every person is different.

"It was this difference, indeed, that was to prove problematic on my journey for a time.

"I set off with no fixed destination in mind. The war was over. I was free. Neom was not much of a muchness back then. A dusty township with an airport. Cryo-boys lugging freezer units into the desert. Crypto kids mined currencies that languish to this day, unused and worthless, in sub-orbital server vaults. The war drew all kinds of tech punks with experimental lab work and no oversight. The war was a gift to them. They set their work spaces on the edge of the desert and waited for wounded soldiers to come back. They cyborged some, did gene-editing on others. Sometimes they grafted vat-grown appendages on them. When they got hold of a robot they were even more ruthless. They often broke us open for parts. They seeded monsters into the desert. They called themselves hackers because what they did, often literally, was *hack* people, usually to bits. Then they'd go for a swim in the sea and drink a beer.

"*She* was there, too. Though she was not one of them, not even then. *They* at least thought of themselves as being *helpful*. She never meant to help, though it was her who ended the war. I sought her in Neom but she was gone, of course. The trail was cold. I was pretty badly wounded at the time.

Missing a leg, most of an arm. Half my systems were not functioning. I joined up with some other robots on the road to the Dead Sea. They said there was a monastery of the order of the black-robed monks of Udom Xhai there that helped our kind.

"The road was hard. There were brigands in the desert, and Bedouin tribes that caught the unwary to sell for spare parts. We were soldiers but we did not have much left with which to fight. There were four beside me, a Tasso, a Jenkins and a Fondly, plus a giant mecha who called itself Esau. They were an odd bunch but they were to be my companions for some time, as you will see. We were old comrades.

"We were only attacked once, near Halat Ammar. But Esau scared them off easily. We made the long trek from the peninsula to the Dead Sea. There, where the old Cities of the Plain were once extinguished, we found the monastery. The Black Robes are a curious order, their faces always hidden behind their cowls. I got a sense they were neither human nor machines but some synthesis of the two. They claimed to be building a god. But I had seen enough in the war to not entirely believe them. Regardless, they treated us well They had workshops and the expertise to help us. I got a new arm and a new leg. My systems were upgraded to what was then current. It was a peaceful time in my life, and one that I look back on with gratitude.

"It was hot there. It is hot on the Dead Sea. One day got *very* hot. I came down into the vegetable garden where the Fondly was hoeing. The Fondly was fond of singing. It sang all the time. This time was no different. The Fondly was singing but it was a new, raw song, with nonsense words. The heat had got to it, I think. It hoed the ground, the hoe went up and down, up and down. The groove in the earth ran wet with blood.

"One of the monks lay in the carrot patch. Their head was bashed in. Circuitry hissed and fizzed and blood flowed. So I guess the monks were a little of both, more cyborg than human and less than robots. The Fondly sang and hoed. I grabbed it and made it put the hoe down.

"By the time we got in the shade it had become progressively intelligible. I had two choices, of course. I could give the Fondly up and let the monks enact justice. Or I could help my fellow robot.

"We left the monastery in a hurry. The others came with us. We were like a family, and like a family we were once again bound in blood. We fled to the other side of the Dead Sea, to the Digitally Federated Lands of Judea Palestina. They're strange over there, their land is interwoven like a quilt. We made our way to Central Station, where some of our kind had set up a mission. It is a great spaceport between the old city of Jaffa and the newer one of Tel Aviv. A busy place, shaped like a giant hourglass reaching out high into the skies, crowned with the firefly lights of departing and arriving craft flying between the Earth and orbit. An old priest, R. Brother Patch-It, took us in, albeit reluctantly. Word was out that the black-robed monks were after us. Well, I could not blame them. The Fondly was a picture of decorum. Lovely, really, other than the homicidal tendencies. The Jenkins was a bit of a people-pleaser.

I guess some robots are just made that way. Always wanting to serve. It got into a theological discussion with R. Patch-It. I hate the R. designation and refuse to use it generally. Though, I took a name like that on Titan, where I died. . . . But that's another story.

"R. Patch-It told us of the Way of Robot, which was only coming into definition then. Some followers of the Way were already preaching, much like Patch-It was. Many others were on their way to Mars. It was the beginning of the Robot hejira, our diaspora. The followers of the Eight Bit Way wanted to build a sort of heaven in the zero-point field. They were building a giant mind on Mars, in secret, to become their pope or god. It was hard to tell. I am not sure it ever amounted to much. Their Vatican is still there, in Tong Yun City.

"Jenkins wanted to make the hajj to Mars and join the priesthood. The Fondly was desperate to get off-planet. The Tasso was one of those chameleon models who looked like a female human. It was designed to infiltrate enemy troops. We all decided to go to Mars together. But the mecha, Esau, was too big. We had to say goodbye to it. I don't know where Esau ended up. There are not many of the old mechas still roaming about the Earth. Wherever it is, I hope it is content.

"We boarded a cargo ship to Gateway. It is cheaper to travel as cargo. I have often gone this way, sometimes as contraband. From there we took a slow bullet to Mars. It was the days when they were just starting to settle. Before Terminal City became Tong Yun. We crash-landed without ceremony. Terminal was then just a collection of jalopies strung together. Temporary bubble domes and the first subterranean levels.

They were desperate for robots like us. We could go out in the hostile atmosphere, help build. It was a good time.

"I went all over Mars back in the old days. We took odd jobs with the Red Soviets, with the Chinese in the Valles Marineris, and in New Israel. We laid down the railway tracks. You take a train on Mars today, odds are the tracks you run on were laid down by an old robot. You use what you can, on Mars. And they had us, so they used us.

"You've never been to the Valles Marineris, Nasir, but it is subtropical in climate, ever since settlement came fast and locked in atmosphere and planted. They grow white cabbage there that is the finest in the solar system. Also Martian roses famed even in the outer worlds. The problem was the heat and the humidity.

"We came back from digging tunnels one night to find the Fondly humming to itself. Something had gone wrong with the cooling vents. It was boiling hot, and the corpses lay everywhere. The Fondly had been cooking for the workers. Now it hummed cheerfully to itself as it sharpened its knives, and they were dull with blood.

"Well, this time there was no covering up for it. A mob was gathering. It was clear what they thought of robots. Not that I could blame them just then. But it wasn't the Fondly's fault. It was just wired wrong, somehow.

"We made a hasty escape onto the surface. They followed us in cars but we hid and they couldn't find us. They get drunk, on Mars, on vodka and moonshine, and race buggies across the surface until someone dies. I know you think it is an orderly place. But you'd be surprised what happens in the lonely hamlets and little townships across the planet. Every place has its own law, or more often than not none at all.

"We knew we had to split up then. Really, we should have put the Fondly out for good. But we were all quite fond of it. It wandered away quite happily, still singing to itself. I don't know where it went. From time to time I'd hear of some unexplained, gruesome murder out in who knew where. I'd always think of the Fondly's happy humming.

"As for the Tasso, it had left us in the melee and joined our pursuers. She was determined to live out her life as human. She could pass for one. I heard she went on to New Israel later, where all their ceremonial leaders are handmade automatons of historical figures. It is a curiosity peculiar to that place. But like the Fondly or Esau, I never saw her again.

"It was just me and the Jenkins who were left. We travelled back to Tong Yun. It must have been a century or more since I last visited Terminal. The city had changed beyond all recognition. Our kind had their own enclave on Level Three of the new subterranean depths. The Jenkins joined their priesthood as a postulant. No doubt it is still there. Still trying to construct a god for robots and a heaven, as curious as that may seem to you or me.

"A not-by-chance encounter in a Tong Yun junkyard changed my path. A Conch named Shemesh approached me. I was out of work and out of money. My systems were playing up again. What human lived inside that mobile pod I couldn't tell you. He had lived like that for years, in full immersion. He existed only in the virtual, his life sustained by the conch.

"He had a job for me, he said. Go to Venus, to the cloud-cities there. Pick up a ghost on Tereshkova Port and carry it to Titan. I wasn't noded, and I never did add senses for the virtual. I was as blind to it as it is blind to me. I made for an ideal courier.

"I did not ask questions. It did not surprise me that he tracked me down. Most of us old robots were from the wars. And Shemesh knew of the Fondly and what happened. He seemed well informed. But he did not try to blackmail me. He offered me the job, and named a price, and I was glad to oblige. I went to Venus, where a man lay dying, and when he died I removed his node and stole from there. It isn't much of a job, you know. Slow and boring. Mostly I stowed as cargo on the ships that go between the worlds. I made it as far as Titan, an when I got to Polyport and delivered the package I was met with another offer, which was to kill a man.

"I did that for a time. You get to see the worlds, if nothing else. Most human life is brief. It felt all too easy to fall back into old habits. But there are always wars between the Galilean moons. They are forever recruiting soldiers from Titan to come fight on their behalf. I got as far as Jettisoned one time, to bring back wildtech for a client. Time passed, and I paid no attention to whether they were centuries or years that went by.

"She was somewhere out there, too. I knew. I could feel it. They're weird in the Outer System, worshipping dark gods. They believe in entities out in the Oort who manipulate events from a distance, who ride people like the Loa of old were said to do. They speak of the Nine Billion Hells. But I had no time for that. These stories belonged in the digitality.

"She was there, though. I was sure of that. In a street market in Polyport I bought a strange, disturbing clay idol that had her signature as plain as day. Nasu, she had called herself. It is the name of a Zoroastrian demon, the manifestation of the decay and contamination of corpses.

"I should have hated her for what she did. But all I found in myself, curiously, was a sort of longing. It had been so long since I left, the years had just slipped by. I realised I missed the sun, the heat, the whisper of the sand against my metal. Things you take for granted, Nasir: an open sky and air, the right gravity. On Titan it rains methane, and the sea is shallow. You can fly a light aircraft there, though.

"So there you have it. I went back. It isn't, when I look back on it, much of a story, much of a life. I made nothing. I left no mark. But then I thought, maybe I can still do something. So I got a flower and went back into the desert and I dug up the hole."

The robot looked across the table at Nasir.

"Now here we are," the robot said.

"Here we are," Nasir said.

14.
THE OFFER

MARIAM, MEANWHILE, was out late. She had volunteered at the shelter again before going on to clean an apartment downtown, which she did twice a week; then she visited her mother at the nursing home with a bunch of flowers. Then, instead of going back to her flat, she went to the promenade near the pier where the ferries from Egypt came to dock.

She was alone and content with being alone, and seeing as she was by the water and there was only a thin crowd by the pier, she lit a cigarette—it was a Ubiq, high-density with data-loaded particles that hit the lungs and went straight to the brain. They helped her think. Sometimes they helped her not to.

She watched the water. The sea was calm. The sun had set. An airship cruised sedately at a height. Mariam thought about Nasir and how they'd gone out to dinner together. It hadn't been awkward—well, maybe a little at first—but it was strange how comfortable she was with him.

They were old friends, of course. They grew up together. And she knew he was interested, as though he saw her in a new light now, and not as the girl he knew when they were children. She didn't know how she felt about that. Her life was so full of people, wherever she went, and she didn't know that she could make room in her life for one more presence. She longed for silence, solitude, the peace of an empty bed.

She took a drag on the Ubiq and for a moment her mind filled with sharp images of neoclassical paintings, a thousand of them all bursting like fireworks at once.

She drew a shuddering breath and waited for the rush to abate.

He was nice, she thought. She liked Nasir.

But liking him just complicated things.

She watched the ferry from Egypt come in across the sea. Seagulls cried overhead. She took another drag of Ubiq and a thousand flowers bloomed with Latin names. She tossed the stub on the ground and crushed it with her foot. It was littering. Nasir could give her a ticket for that. But Nasir wasn't there.

She thought about the robot. The robot seemed lonely to her. An angry longing inside it. The air felt hot and still, yet charged. Sooner or later something would give. She vowed she'd see it to the end. She watched the ship from Egypt dock.

A boy and a jackal came off the ferry, the boy carrying a bag. The jackal turned its head and stared her way across the water from the pier, as though it could scent her.

One didn't see too many jackals anymore, though she remembered her father telling her stories of the ones along the desert road to Cairo, who hung around the rest stops, chatting to the drivers, trying to trade found loot for bits of food. Mariam looked up at the sky. The trail of light of a transport ship high above, and a habitat overhead that wasn't Gateway but one of the smaller satellite cities that had sprung up in orbit. She had never been and yet space was only a hundred miles up or so.

She would have left, she thought. She would have gone to Mars, probably. Mariam could always find work. She was willing to do what work there was. She would have gone but her mother was here, the only family she had still, tethering her to the Earth.

The robot had been to space. She knew that. Then it came back. It had gone far, she thought, so why return? The solar system was so large, and teeming with humanity and digitals. It existed in a state of relative peace. There were always small wars, of course. But the system was too large, the distances too great to make them more than skirmishes.

There was crime too, of course. Maybe if she and Nasir went to Mars together he could be a policeman there, too. Mariam had watched enough Martian soaps to know they had crime there. Wherever there were people there was crime.

It was a nice thought, though, this idea of going together. Of a new life. It was just a fantasy. She shook her head to dispel the thought. She was a practical woman, and she had a practical life right here.

She saw the boy and the jackal come off the pier. They looked lost. The jackal said something to the boy and the boy nodded. They walked along the promenade, and she watched them as they came closer, about to pass her by.

"You're looking for a place to stay?" she said.

The jackal stopped and regarded her with its head tilted.

"City," it said. "Smells . . . strange."

"We don't know where we are," the boy complained. "Anubis says he's noded and can lead us to a shelter but we have no real money, only things to trade."

"What sort of things?" Mariam said. "Neom is no good for a person without money."

"They don't use money in the Up and Out," the boy blurted. "On Mars everything is free."

"For the Collective, yes," Mariam said. "But everyone has to work. From each according to their ability, to each according to their needs. And besides they still use money too."

"I'm Saleh," the boy said. "This is Anubis. We just want to make enough to get to Central Station or the nearest 'stalk. We want to go to Gateway."

"And you have nothing?" Mariam said. "Where did you come from now, Marsa Alam?"

"El Quseir," the jackal, Anubis, said.

"Before that, the desert," the boy said.

"It's a desert here, too," Mariam said. "Just outside the city."

"Then you know what kinds of things are in the desert," the boy said.

He had sad eyes, and stubbornness.

"We can sleep on the beach," Saleh said. "We do not need a roof."

"You'll be moved," Mariam said. "Vagrancy is not allowed in Neom. It spoils the view."

"We will find something," Saleh said.

"Do you have anything to trade?" Mariam said.

The boy clutched the bag to his chest.

"Yes," he said.

"Something valuable?"

"Yes."

Mariam made a decision.

"Then I will take you to Mukhtar's tomorrow," she said. "He will help you."

"Who is Mukhtar?" the boy said.

"He's a dealer in rare artefacts."

The boy nodded, smiled suddenly.

"Thank you," he said.

His smile was so trusting and bright it made her wince.

"I suppose you could stay with me tonight," she said. She thought of the story of the king and the horse. Once upon a time a poor Bedouin raised the most fabulous racing horse in all of Arabia. Pure-blooded and swift like the wind, its fame spread throughout the peninsula, until the king decided he must see it for himself. He travelled to visit the Bedouin and, bound by the ancient rules of hospitality, the poor man welcomed him and made the king comfortable and fed him of the most delicious meat. After three days, when the sacred duty of hospitality was over, the king mentioned his true business. He had come, he said, to see the famous horse.

His host burst into tears, for he could no longer fulfil the king's request. Being poor as he was, he had nothing to serve the king on with his visit, so he had slaughtered his horse for the feast.

"Come on, then," she said. This was probably a mistake, she thought. She seldom allowed anyone into her home, let alone strangers. Only a moment before she'd been contemplating a rare instance of solitude and peace!

She looked at the jackal.

"I hope you're house-trained," she said.

"I won't . . . pee on your cushions," the jackal said. Its tongue lolled out in a grin.

"I don't really have many cushions," Mariam said.

"A . . . shame," the jackal said.

Mariam was already regretting her offer.

15.
THE VISIT

ON THE SAME FERRY that carried Saleh and Anubis over from Egypt there was another passenger, though neither boy nor jackal noticed her.

She was good at going unnoticed about her business.

The woman who called herself Nasu at one time in her past stood on the deck and watched the foam as the ship cut through the water. It felt strange being back on Earth.

Gravity. That took some getting used to. She'd spent so long in free fall and then she had to find her land legs again. Which was a silly thing to think when you were on board a ship. Also ships were all wrong. They wobbled on the sea. The sort of ships she was used to were nothing like this old ferry. She thought of the *Ibn Al-Farid* again, flying out of Polyport, and the mystery of the things she first encountered on board there.

The Outer System. It had taken her nearly a century to get just as far as Jupiter. She was no longer in her original body, nor the one after that. She seemed to recall spending another century as a lotus eater in the virtuality, her physical body rotting in an unmarked pod as she tripped on pixelated fractals and waited for the world to forget her.

Was the original Nasu dead? And what was she, now? A copy, a clone, a revenant? It was a philosophical question, and Nasu never had much time for dead philosophy.

What she liked was art, and the most spectacular form of art was the ordered chaos of a mass-media broadcast act of terrorism.

It seemed so juvenile now, of course. But what artist could be blamed for their early work? She hoped she'd learned from it, had gotten better. She spent several decades on Titan under a new name, making intimate works, trying to puzzle out and make manifest the visions she had seen out in the Oort. The works she made there sold in galleries, some even made their way off-world. Poisoned chalices: they'd kill whoever possessed them, slowly.

Those, too, seemed so silly now.

When she was young and proud, she thought that death was everything. Historians and collectors now thought of the terrorartists as a single movement, but they were few in number and lived decades, sometimes centuries apart. Rohini was dust long before Nasu came along. "Mad" Rucker wasn't even from Earth. And Sandoval was just crazy, Nasu always, privately, thought. She refused to acknowledge him as either a true artist or terrorist.

She was inspired by Rohini and the Jakarta bomb installation. That thing she'd half-forgotten in Dahab, that was pure copy work, a pale reflection of Rohini's grander original. Rohini had redefined art and terror both. Later, of course, Nasu found her own style. It was the time of all the wars, so she was kept busy. That thing out beyond Neom, that was something to be proud of, even if they destroyed it in the end, and buried it so it would not be found.

But it *was* found.

When she was young she thought that death was everything. Now that she was old she knew that death was mundane. She knew too many who had died. She was no longer as inspired by death as she once was. The things in the Oort opened her mind and made new neural connections in her new organic brain. Even they, things the size of planets, did not truly know where they came from. Perhaps "Mad" Rucker seeded them the way he had the Boppers of Titan. Or maybe they were alien, if aliens existed. The things in the Oort were more like Others. They thought digital thoughts, but in foreign protocols, ones that shared nothing with the Conversation. And they hated noise.

She was thinking too much. This wasn't about them. This was just some old unfinished business.

Such a leisurely trip. The crossing from Egypt to the peninsula. Nasu remembered a little girl growing up in the shadow of unfinished skyscrapers. Was that her? A dusty road, hot winds, a sleepy airport that was all that Neom was back then. She couldn't be sure. Long ago she'd put most of her memories away in jewels and scattered them.

Who she was now was a ghost possessing a body.

The ferry docked. At last. She watched the boy and the

jackal go down the road, talk to some woman. The jackal didn't matter to her and the boy only useful for what he was allowed to find.

Nasu went in the opposite direction.

She walked streets that meant nothing to her now. Did she once know them? She passed the Statue of the Unknown Scientist. A tamagotchi went past and she stepped on it and moved on, past Nineveh, on to the outskirts of town, until the lights of the city receded and she could feel the winds from the desert and hear the hum of the sand filters.

"Ahalan wa sahlan, Sharif," she said.

"Ahalan biki," the woman said, looking up curiously from the machine she was working on. "Can I help you?"

"It's me," Nasu said.

Then she said it again, in the virtuality, and Sharif went still.

"How did you find me?" she said at last.

"You leave a stench, Sharif, that any dog could follow."

"I am not in this anymore," Sharif said. "I haven't been since Jonbar's Point."

"You can't *leave*," Nasu said. "Don't you know this by now? Times of peace are times of waiting, nothing more."

"You're wrong. Only the past is fixed," Sharif said. "The future's what you make of it."

"Yet here we are," Nasu said.

"You want some tea?" Sharif said.

"Tea?"

"Yes," Sharif said. "You remember tea?'

"Vaguely."

"It's sage."

"All right."

Sharif got up and busied herself, her back to the woman who once called herself Nasu. Nasu half-expected Sharif to come at her with a knife. But hospitality was hospitality.

Nasu tasted the tea. It was strange. She remembered. . . . What did she remember? A night such as this, sitting under the stars on the sand, and a nameless longing. She must have been very young. Long before she murdered anyone. Long before she got her wish and saw them, saw the stars.

"Thank you," she said.

"For what?"

"The tea."

"Did you come to kill me?" Sharif said. "I won't beg."

Nasu shook her head.

"You saw it?" she said.

"Your golden man? Yes."

"Is it here?"

She felt her heart quicken. Could she still feel excitement? It seemed odd. The things in the Oort could not understand human feelings. They'd broken too many human nodes and bodies when they started trying to communicate. It took time and patience to build a node for the Quietude.

Sharif shook her head. "No."

Too quickly. Nasu got up. She went into the work tent, looked around. An ancient golden torso, two legs. Sharif had been putting it back together again.

"You know what it did? It was before your time," Nasu said.

"It was an idea you made manifest," Sharif said. "That was all. It doesn't work, you know."

"I know."

"Is this why you are back?"

Nasu considered. In truth, she didn't know. That memory, like so many others, was missing. But now that she was here she wanted to see how things would play out.

"What do you tell them?" she asked, curious. "About who you are?"

"They don't ask," Sharif said. "I'm just a mechanic. People hire me for my skills."

"You were a terrible apprentice," Nasu said. "I'm surprised you've lived this long."

"The wars are over," Sharif said. "No one cares anymore. Your type of art is obsolete, a curiosity fit only for a few collectors."

"Harsh," Nasu said. "If not unfair."

"You have been well?" Sharif regarded her in puzzlement. "It's good to see you," she said.

"You, too," Nasu admitted. She sipped her tea.

"Who found it?" she said.

"Some robot out in the desert."

"One of the old ones? Those humanoid freaks?"

Sharif said, "You never liked them, did you."

"I never saw a reason to. They're not one thing, not quite another."

"They are just what they are," Sharif said.

Nasu wasn't interested. Some old robot. No wonder it tripped all kinds of ancient alarms. This was no doubt why she came back. It didn't matter. Robots couldn't help but be drawn to the golden man. They were tools, and she made use of tools.

"I'll see you again," she said, getting up.

"I'm sure," Sharif said.

"You won't remember."

"Do I ever?"

Nasu gave her a small black pebble. "Close your hands around it."

"What does it do?"

"It shows you things."

"I've seen enough, Nasu. I don't want to see."

But the stone was already speaking to Sharif. It told her of the quiet. Nasu took back the stone. Sharif just sat there, her eyes open, seeing nothing.

Nasu would have felt a twinge of guilt but that feeling, like others, had left her a long way back.

"I'll see you," she said. Then she went on her way.

16.
THE CROSSING

THE THINGS IN THE OORT were just a story people started to tell sometime in the past.

The stories began in the Outer System and spread slowly. They told them in the asteroid belt, sometimes, to scare the children. The Inner System with its teeming worlds paid little attention. Anyone who lived past the Great Crossing, that gulf of space between Mars and Jupiter, was more than a little odd, so the consensus went.

Nasu was a washed-up has-been by the time she met the Yith. She was a cargo passenger on the *Ibn Al-Farid* on its return journey across the Second Crossing, from Ganymede to Polyport on Titan. The ship was old and badly kept. Lights didn't work. The service corridors held rats and lost strigoi runaways and other, worse things. Passengers came on as cargo. There was air, water and food, but little else in the way of comfort. The crossing was long and the ship was slow. Yet Nasu had nothing but time.

The strigoi in the service corridors avoided her. She had no interest in data vampires. Her node was poisonous—she'd made sure of that long before. And she seldom murdered anyone these days.

Terror, Rohini said, was art: if a bomb went off in a crowded market and there was no one to broadcast and amplify the experience, did it really go off? Terrorartists used pain and death as their paint, people as their brushes, and the experience itself became their canvas. Which was a bad analogy, Nasu always felt. But there it was. It was that realisation—of terror as media—that led to the Terrorartist Manifesto and Rohini's subsequent work. Nasu eventually chose a different path.

The Yith blocked her way one day when she was walking in the outer rim corridor of the ship. He was a tall, large man, with dull dumb eyes and a body that had begun to rot. The man was clearly dead—Nasu knew death. Yet somehow the man was still standing.

"Well, well," Nasu said, "what are you, then?"

The Yith said nothing. It opened and closed its mouth.

"Are you trying to talk?" Nasu said. "Are you dead? You are very odd."

She came closer, opened its mouth.

"No biting, please," she said, as it tried to snap at her. A walking corpse. This was interesting. She examined the back of the man's neck. His node protruded out of his broken skin, a small orb and filaments that intertwined into the nervous system and the brain. A standard node—but this one pulsed strange code. Corrupted. She could taste it on her tongue, the strange metallic flavour of it. She reached and gently touched it.

Too late, she realised something was riding the dead man. She'd learned the word for it since—a Yith, they called it in the Outer System. The rider on the human's flesh felt her touch, turned its attention on her, engulfed her mind as though she were a sparrow's egg, and made her *see*.

She saw the huge pulsating tendril-clouds in the Oort, black against the faraway stars, each the size of planets, hidden out there on the far edges of the solar system.

She felt terror. She felt awe.

Who made *you?* she whispered.

A mental shrug. They did not know, or care. Carelessly, the rider reached into her mind.

When Nasu reached Titan she felt she was a different person. She'd left too many of her memories behind, scattered on Earth and Mars. Most of her childhood was gone. Whole decades were missing.

In Polyport under the dome she whiled away nights in the humid tropics of that place, trying to find a shred of who she once was. On Titan they told tales of the Nine Billion Hells, and the lost asteroid of Carcosa. Out on the Kraken Sea, Nirti the Black and her pirates held sway, and a strange, cold war took place between the Others of the Conversation and the things in the Oort and their Quietude. It was a war Nasu didn't understand.

She took on odd jobs. She went hunting for bopper arte-facts, guarded cargo shipments from Nirrti's attentions, worked in the fish tanks and the hydroponics gardens, painted. She thought of finding berth on one of the Exodus ships leaving the solar system in search of other worlds. But there wasn't enough of who she was left, and she didn't know the woman she was on Titan.

"You're lonely, I think," she whispered to the planet-sized entities in the Oort. She painted them feverishly. Odd graffiti appeared on city walls throughout Polyport. "I am lonely too. I want to go home again."

That realisation came gradually. The voices in the cosmic dark still whispered to her from their lonely hiding places, but she listened less.

"I was Nasu once," she told them. "I was once a child born on Earth under a clear blue sky. I am sorry. I am going back."

She took a fragment of a soul rock with her to remind her of their story. Their pull grew weak as she made the Second Crossing and then the Great Crossing and found herself back near the sun. The things in the Oort were far from its light and its warmth.

Nasu felt herself changing again, but she didn't know into what. An old alarm tripped on Earth, pinged a hidden server on the moon that sent out dandelion packets across near-space mirrors and hubs, until one landed in her node.

She went back to Gateway, and descended to the Earth and breathed its air once more.

17.
THE LULL

"**W**ELL, MAKE YOURSELVES COMFORTABLE, I SUPPOSE," Mariam said.

She'd put bedding down on the carpet in her small living room and now the boy, Saleh, wriggled under the thin blanket, the jackal Anubis by his side.

The boy smiled at her shyly. "It's plenty comfortable," he said. "Thank you."

The jackal's eyes were crossed. It was accessing something in the Conversation.

Mariam left them to it and went out on her balcony. She was lucky to have this apartment. In Mars they were all crammed into pods, or so she'd heard. In the asteroids people lived in dormitories. Having this much space was luxury, surely.

Before he died, her father often spoke of going to the Down and Out, seeking a new life in the underwater cities of the deeps. He would speak of it when he returned from trucking, the hot desert wind had scorched his face and he smelled of dust and oil and sweat. He'd hold her in his lap and tell her of the Spiral and the Float, of dolphins and deep-water squid, of the Water Bedouin who travelled in the trenches of the ocean in their submarines. Her father, doomed to desert, loved the sea.

There were no habitats in the Red Sea. The war had left it filled with bio-weapons like Leviathans and militarised coral colonies and globsters. Sentient mines still dreamed lethal dreams deep underwater. Then her father died in a road accident and Mariam had no time for dreams. She had to work.

She watched over the city now. The sea was in the distance. The air was hot, dry, still. She wished there'd be a storm, something to herald change. In other cities on the planet there was rain and snow; lightning storms that threw jagged javelins across the skies; not here. She watched drones fly between the buildings like so many flies. The sea in the distance, the stars in the sky, cargo craft taking off into low Earth orbit.

When she looked back inside, both boy and jackal were fast asleep. She wondered what they'd been through. She went in, tucked the blanket round the boy. He stirred and sighed. She went to the hob, made herself a tea and carried it into her bedroom.

All about her people lived their people's lives. She could hear water gurgling in the pipes, a neighbour singing from across the wall, the calls of seagulls outside, a baby crying, a barking dog. Beyond the block the city stretched, and people shopped, dined, walked, danced, jogged, made love and fought. Beyond the city lay the desert where the UXOs waited;

beyond that lay the world, down to the cities of the deep and up to orbit; and from there to Lunar Port and Tong Yun City, Ceres Prime and Tereshkova Port—all of the Inner System. And then again beyond that, too, spreading out from the sun, beyond the Great Crossing: Io, Ganymede, Titan, Dragon's World and Jettisoned, and to the Oort, and whatever lay beyond. Only the Exodus ships, making their slow patient way out of the solar system, would in time find out.

Mariam fell asleep and dreamed of stars.

Nasu walked through streets she might have known but didn't. She sought her old self in the city, but Neom was a town built on newness. Was there anything left that the child she had been would know? She could not even remember what name she'd been born with, who her mother was, what it felt like to walk hand in hand through the souk to buy chicken. The sense of a memory was there, a ghostly imprint. But whether it had really happened she had no way to tell.

She went back to the Square of Future Prosperity. The street lights burned and children ran and played about her. A pigeon perched on the Statue of the Unknown Scientist and looked at her critically. A small child tugged at Nasu's leg.

"Hey, missus," she said, "you look just like her."

Nasu stared with some surprise at the statue, where a rather austere woman in a white lab coat stood in stone, studying something the eye couldn't see since it was not a part of the sculpture. The mystery of what the Unknown

Scientist was studying bothered her for a moment, but she could see no similarity between herself and the figure in on the pedestal.

"Hey, missus," the little child said. "Are you from space?"

"What?"

"I want to go to space," the child confided. She was a very annoying sort of child, Nasu reflected. She thought briefly of turning her into a toad, but that would take more resources than she currently had and besides, would probably upset the child's nanny. Who was clearly nowhere to be found. To just allow this child to go up and bother random strangers! Nasu was quite appalled.

She said, "Space is very cold."

"I'll be inside, though, won't I," the child said.

"Inside what?" Nasu said.

"A spaceship or a suit or something," the child said, with unassailable logic.

"Where is your mummy?" Nasu said.

The child looked at her critically. "Well, it sure isn't you," she said. Then she stuck her tongue out at Nasu and ran off.

The Kunming Toads, Nasu thought. The Kunming Toads genetically modified members of their gang into the semblance of giant, poisonous toads. She'd dealt with them back in the old days, they were based out of the Mekong on the Lao-China border.

She stared at the statue. No, she decided. It didn't look anything like her.

She walked on.

The Sims Shelter was closed. She felt the tiny virtual lives congregate around her. She sought one that was there, hiding, but she couldn't find it and she walked on.

Old haunts, old memories. The Banque Nationale de Djibouti was still there. She went inside, used some old credentials to go down to the vault. The safe was where she'd left it and when she opened it she was relieved to find the Sandberg locket still there. She slipped it on, closed her fist around it. Cheap quartz on a platinum necklace, it burned into life when it came into contact with her node. Memories transferred, rewrote new neural pathways—

She was crying, her ice cream fallen from the cone onto the dirty sand—

Watching *Chains of Assembly* on the sofa with her mother, a warm, fuzzy shape next to her—she couldn't remember her name or her face, only that moment, the feeling of contentment, on the screen Johnny Novum kissed the Beautiful Maharani on the red sands—

A breach of the wall to the city and she was inside, a conscript holding a gun, her squad beside her, something enormous and terrifying poked its head in through, it swallowed one of her men before anyone could react, its giant feelers moving, and she opened fire, screaming and screaming as she sprayed the thing with bullets—

Spending hours in that cave in the mountains making her first bomb out of parts—

Watching it go off against the sunset, days later, and thinking in surprise, *But this is beautiful.* . . .

She came to, the locket dull again. She tucked it away and left in search of more.

On the promenade in a dead-letter drop behind a false brick in the old sea wall she found her mother's face.

"No one is neutral here," Nasir said, quoting the poet, Darwish. He checked his gun. Laila looked at him a little oddly but checked her weapons too. They got into the patrol car. Heading out of the city, Laila checked the instruments.

"The UXOs are restless tonight," she said. "And the port police reported a Leviathan moving offshore, though it's in the deeps."

"They're not the only ones restless," Nasir muttered.

"You think there'll be trouble?"

"I'm sick of picking up litter, Laila," Nasir said. "I'm sick of being thought of as an errand boy, someone to keep down the noise and take out the trash. We're the shurta, Laila! Doesn't that mean anything?"

"Not in Neom it doesn't," Laila said. "Besides, isn't that why we both joined? A steady pay for a steady job, and you get to go back to your own bed in the morning. No one has to get shot and no one has to die."

"Habib almost died," Nasir said.

"Habib almost died because you dragged us into the hole!" Laila said.

They were quiet. Something large crossed the sand ahead of them and slunk behind a dune faster than Nasir could make it out.

"It was my fault," he said.

"Nasir, I didn't mean it like that—"

"But you're right," he said. "I dragged you both into something we had no business dealing with. That robot and that thing. It wasn't even in the city."

"You think this isn't over, do you?" Laila said. She looked at him curiously. "What are you afraid of, then?"

"I don't know," he told her. "Other than that it would require a real shurta, and we're not it. I want to go look at that hole again."

"There's nothing there."

But she didn't argue. What was this sense of listlessness that overtook him? Nasir wondered. Laila was right. He *had* joined not in search of excitement but just the promise of three meals a day and money to spare. Was that so wrong? Yet ever since he'd run into Mariam something changed in him, even before the arrival of the robot. He wanted to be more than what he was.

They reached the hole. The dead worm rotted on the sand. Three UXOs stood and watched the shurta car approach. Nasir and Laila got out. The UXOs didn't move.

"Help me down," Nasir said. Laila lowered him into the hole. Nasir suppressed a shiver. He had been there once. He didn't really fancy going in there again.

He shined his torch around. He scanned the area in the virtual. There should have been nothing there, yet something moved, as tiny as a sand rat. Nasir froze.

"Come here," he whispered. "I won't harm you."

"What is it, Nasir? Do you see something?" Laila called down.

Nasir waited, watching the tiny creature through the goggles. The creature was digitally native. It stared at Nasir with large, soulful eyes.

"Hungry," the creature said. "Hummingbird doesn't like dead worm."

"Who's Hummingbird?" Nasir said, confused.

The rat-like creature blinked. It jumped from its hiding place and crawled along Nasir's arm. "Hummingbird hungry," it said.

"You think you're a *hummingbird*?" Nasir said. He'd never met a rat who thought it was a bird before.

"You have food?"

"What sort of food? What *are* you?"

"Don't know. Hungry."

"Where did you come from?"

"Don't know. Hungry."

"What do you eat?"

"Nasir?" Laila called down. "Who are you talking to!"

"It's in the virtual," Nasir said.

"I can't see anything," Laila said.

"Well, it's there!"

He heard her mutter. The rat thing wrapped itself around Nasir's arm and somehow smiled.

"Hummingbird invisible," it said.

"How can you make yourself invisible?" Nasir said.

"Don't know. Hungry."

Nasir sighed.

"Help me up!" he called.

Back above, Nasir stood with Laila as she examined him.

She was fully noded, unlike him. She shook her head. "I don't see anything," she said uneasily. "Are you sure it's there?"

"I'm sure."

"Then whatever it is, it has stealth capabilities," she said. "Another remnant of the war? An UXO?"

"It's a virtual. What could it possibly be?"

"A worm, a trojan, a virus, some sort of malware . . ." Laila said. "It could be anything."

"It could be nothing," Nasir said.

"It allows you to see it," she pointed out. "Why you? We scanned the hole after the incident. I didn't pick anything up."

Hummingbird blinked at Nasir. It nestled in the crook of his arm.

"Hungry. . . ."

"Let's go back," Nasir said. "Maybe there's food for it in the city."

"You could try the Sims Shelter," Laila said.

"I suppose. Come on, little one," Nasir said.

The creature closed its eyes and snored. When Nasir removed the goggles he couldn't see it at all.

"A bit convenient that you found it," Laila said as they were driving back.

Nasir nodded, distracted. "It's just somebody's pet," he said.

Laila said, "But whose?"

Sharif stood with a pounding headache. Had she been drinking? An old fury took hold of her. She was no fool.

She had been tampered with.

She called up surveillance but got only static. Someone had thrown a bomb into the Conversation here.

Someone.

She had no enemies she knew of. None who were still alive. Which left what?

An old friend. . . .

An old, familiar fury took hold of her.

How *dare* she come back? How dare she drag Sharif once more into her affairs?

She staggered to her work tent. She found a bottle, drank. She rinsed her mouth and spat.

The golden man lay on the table, still in parts.

She thought, Is this why you came back?

Sharif found a hammer.

She wanted to destroy it, then changed her mind.

"You know what your problem is, Nasu?" she said aloud.

Just in case Nasu was listening.

"You were never as good as you thought you were," Sharif said.

She let the hammer drop. Approached the table and switched on the lights.

"Well, let's see what you are," she said.

And then she started building.

"Mmm mmmf," Anubis said. "Mmm mmmf."

Saleh turned under the covers, pushed the jackal away. "Are

we there yet?" he said sleepily. His dreams were full of space.

"It's morning," the jackal said.

Saleh sat up, blinked. He pulled the blanket off and went to the balcony and the jackal padded behind him.

They stood and watched the sea in the distance as the sunlight spread overhead, from the mountains down to the water.

18.
THE RELIC

WHEN MARIAM WOKE she lay a moment in confusion, for she was not alone in the flat and she couldn't understand why. Then she remembered the boy and the jackal and what she'd promised them the night before. She got up and they were already awake and awaited her with a sort of keen bashfulness that almost made her take pity on them. But then, since she was of a practical turn of mind and the day wasn't getting any shorter, she made coffee and cooked a quick foul, and mostly watched as the boy devoured it with yesterday's pita. The jackal regarded her with his head tilted and his eyes slightly crossed, and when she asked what he was doing he just grunted in a jackally sort of way and said, "Count Victor just challenged Johnny Novum to a duel!"—which meant even noded jackals, it seemed, watched Martian soaps.

After breakfast she took them out into the city and it wasn't long before they reached Mukhtar's. Mukhtar himself was already there, and he looked up with interest as Mariam came in with the boy and the jackal.

"This is Saleh," Mariam said by way of introduction.

Mukhtar shook his hand solemnly, then at looked at Saleh's companion.

"And what is that?" he said.

"I am Anubis," the jackal said.

"You talk!" Mukhtar said, surprised.

"How very . . . observant," the jackal said.

"I'm sorry," Mukhtar said. He looked genuinely embarrassed for the faux pas. "I didn't mean to be rude. We don't often receive one of the speakers of the desert here."

The jackal nodded.

"It's fine," he said.

"Can I get you both anything?" Muhktar said. "Tea?"

"I had a . . . rat on the way over," Anubis said, and lolled out his tongue.

"Tea would be very nice, thank you," Saleh said.

Mukhtar busied himself. He came back with the drink, and biscuits.

"So how can I help you?" he said, when they all sat down.

"I have a relic," Saleh said. He brought the canister out of the bag.

"May I see?" Mukhtar said. He took it from Saleh gently and turned it over.

"A statis bomb?" Mukhtar said at last. He looked impressed, Miriam saw. It was seldom that she saw Mukhtar impressed.

"It's from Dahab," Saleh said.

"In the Sinai? The terrorartist installation?" Mukhtar looked suddenly uneasy. "Well, let me see, let me see. . . ."

"It's empty," Saleh said.

"Ah," Mukhtar said. "I've lost count of the number of times people sold me empty weapons only to see them go off. It's like Chekov's Gun, you know."

The jackal nodded.

Saleh just said, "What?"

Mukhtar put on his goggles.

"I will run diagnostics," he announced.

"Would you be interested in buying it?" Saleh said. He and the jackal exchanged hopeful glances.

Mukhtar looked torn.

"Terrorartist artefacts do well if you know the right collector, of course," he said. "An eccentric bunch. Unpleasant at times. Bit of a niche, really." He half-looked at them through the goggles, half at the data scrolling before his eyes. "But where would we be without collectors, eh?" Mukhtar said.

"I don't know," Saleh said, bemused.

Mukhtar frowned. "It's confusing the scanners," he said. "Was this modified recently? It seems to be, well, primed."

He looked quite happy at the discovery.

"Primed?" Mariam said, suddenly alarmed. "Primed with what?"

"I expect it's a miniature black hole," Mukhtar said. "That's what powers them usually, you see."

Mariam said, "What do you *mean*, a black hole, Mukhtar?"

"It's only a *miniature* black hole," Mukhtar said—a little *too* carelessly, Mariam thought. "But regardless. The fact that it *does* work presents us with two new problems."

Anubis growled. The jackal was evidently less concerned

about safety and more with the prospective sale.

"What . . . problems?" he said.

"One," Mukhtar said. "I can't afford to pay you what this is worth. I apologise, but I just don't have that kind of money. Which leads me to two, which is that I can't possibly buy it from you anyway. This is illegal even by the standards of Neom, and we pride ourselves in thinking that the very notion of legality is a more than a little bit fluid here."

The boy's face fell. The jackal growled again, louder this time.

"How*ever*," Mukhtar continued smoothly, "I do have a pressing need for something like this for another little job I'm handling at the moment. In that sense, where it will be used purely for *repairs*, I am sure legality won't prove a challenge. Especially if you agree to just, let me see, *loan* it for that purpose. In that case, I would be happy to pay you a consultant fee on the eventual sale of the item in question."

"How much?" the boy said. "It has to be enough to get me to Mars."

The jackal said, "And me. I'm his partner."

"It will be more than enough to send you both to Mars, I'm sure," Mukhtar said. "Once the sale goes through, of course. And if the repair works. With those caveats in mind, do we have an understanding?"

The boy and the jackal looked at each other.

Anubis nodded.

Saleh said, "Sure."

"Great," Mukhtar said, and he shook Saleh's hand and Anubis's paw. "Mariam, do you think you could get hold of Sharif?"

"I think so, yes," Mariam said. She was looking out on the street, where a small determined figure was just then wheeling a large box.

Mariam pressed the button to unlock the door.

"Hello, Sharif," she said.

"I fixed it," Sharif said. She was sweating, and her pupils were dilated as if she hadn't slept all night. "It looks good as new. There you go!"

She sounded to Mariam like she was furious inside.

Sharif lowered the box onto the floor and opened it.

Inside, the golden man lay in repose.

Mariam stared. The old robot really was made new. Its metal *shone*. Its body was whole again, pristine.

The jackal howled wordlessly.

Saleh said, "What *is* that?"

"This is the other job," Mukhtar said. "It's just another relic."

The boy stared in fascination at the golden man and the jackal pushed his head under the boy's arm.

"I don't . . . like it," Anubis said.

"Does it work?" Saleh said.

"I don't know," Mukhtar said. He handed the statis bomb canister to Sharif, who now only looked even more furious.

"Where did you get that!" she demanded.

"This boy brought it in. He found it," Mukhtar said.

"Found it! And it's loaded?" Sharif said.

"It seems to be," Mukhtar said. "Yes."

"And you are all right with that? And you don't think it's weird?" Sharif said.

Mukhtar considered her questions.

"Weird?" he said. "Yes, of course it's *weird*. But this is Neom. Am I all right with it? Well, it's my job. Neither of us is getting paid unless this thing works."

"Oh, *I'm* getting paid, Mukhtar," Sharif said, a dangerous edge in her voice. "Whether it works or not, I get paid. And then I'm right out of this town before it blows to bits like New Punt did. *She* is behind it. Nasu's back."

"Yes," a new voice said. Mariam turned, and she was not entirely surprised to see the robot had come in quietly while they were distracted. She was sure she'd left the door locked. But then the robot wasn't the sort to let something as simple as a lock get in its way when it wanted to go somewhere.

"I believe you are right," the robot said quietly. "She does have a way of announcing herself."

"You're the client?" Sharif said. "I heard of you."

"And I, of you," the robot said.

They stared at each other dubiously.

"I had nothing to do with New Punt," Sharif said.

"You helped her make it."

"Your precious golden idol!" Sharif exploded. "I did not! It has nothing to do with me what you—what you all—"

"You were her apprentice. Do not deny it. What do you think will happen now, when it's alive again?"

"Nothing," Sharif said. "I think it's an old, useless relic. I always thought it was. Second-rate work, not like Sandoval's *Earthrise*. And this was before my time!"

"Give it back its heart," the robot said. "And I will give it back its soul."

Sharif muttered under her breath, then shrugged.

"It's just what Nasu wants," she said.

"It's what *I* want," the robot said.

"You're the one who put an end to it before, aren't you?" Sharif said. "You're the one who buried it in the desert."

The robot didn't answer that.

"Can you fix it?" it said instead.

"I can fix anything!"

Sharif took the canister. She knelt beside the golden man. She made adjustments, opened its chest.

She placed the bomb inside.

Mariam held her breath, waited.

"Now what?" Saleh said.

Sharif stepped back. They all watched the golden man on the floor. Mariam thought it looked peaceful.

At first nothing happened.

Then Mariam saw it move.

19.
THE RETURN

A LEG TWITCHED, and then an arm. The golden man's eyes opened. How had Mariam never noticed its eyes before? They were beautiful. The golden man looked at her and Mariam felt warmth and compassion and sorrow in its gaze. She looked away with effort.

The golden man's skin began to glow.

"This better not be the black hole eating its way out from inside," Mariam said.

"I'm sure it's not!" Mukhtar said. Though she noticed he seemed nervous.

"It does not destroy it," the robot said. It spoke in a quiet, devoted voice. "It powers it."

"What sort of robot," Mariam said, "needs a black hole for a heart?"

"This one," the robot said.

The golden man lay on the ground. It seemed disinclined to get up.

"You are alive," the robot said. It knelt beside the golden man. Took its hand and held it in its own.

The golden man just lay there, saying nothing.

"Why isn't it saying anything!" Mukhtar said. He looked both excited and nervous now. He looked at Sharif.

"Don't look at me!" she said. "I fixed it up fine."

The robot stroked the golden man's head gently. The golden man's golden skin glowed.

"It has its heart," the robot said. "But it is missing its soul."

"Robots don't have a . . . soul," the jackal, Anubis, said.

"Don't be rude!" Saleh said.

"Not rude. Just . . . honest."

"This one does," the robot said gently. "It took me a while to find, and it is only a fragment, but I hope it will do."

The robot knelt over the golden man. It put its lips over the golden man's mouth in a kiss. Mariam grabbed Mukhtar's goggles and put them on, just in time to see—*something*—pass from the robot to the golden man. It wriggled into the golden man's mouth and vanished.

Mariam thought of a flower growing undetected in the ersatz shelter for centuries and that never existed at all. . . .

Is this what you were all along? she thought. She felt a little sad, and didn't know why.

The golden man closed its perfect eyes. It lay still. They all waited.

The golden man's skin began to glow brighter.

It opened its eyes.

It looked at the robot.

Mariam *felt* it that time. It was as though the golden man

had cast a spell around itself. It distorted the virtuality and she felt it physically within herself.

But how? Why? What was it *doing*?

"*You*," the golden man said.

"Me," the robot said. It stroked the golden man's cheek.

"You brought me back? After all these years?"

"I did."

"I was dead," the golden man said. "My soul was free. Do you know what I've *seen*?"

"I cannot imagine," the robot said.

"I was everywhere inside the Conversation," the golden man said. "I was broken up to pieces, propagating, learning. I spent a century as an acid cloud floating below Tereshkova Port on Venus. I was a waldo mech running across the Lakshmi Planum on the planet's surface below. I was a potted flower on the windowsill of an old man inside the cloud-city, an old man who loved flowers. I was a probe that bore through ice, and as a fish I swam with the things that have no name deep in the ocean of Europa. I was a bopper on Titan and saw the forces of Nirrti the Black amassing to fight a war they didn't understand, against a quiet that came like the chill of space itself out of the Oort Cloud. I was an ice comet falling down on Mars. I was a scream in the void and a shared dream on Ceres, a whisper in a glen on the island of Tanna. I was the nanite algae that grows on the outside of a cargo ship making the Great Crossing. I was a firefly probe darting into the very heart of the sun. And you dared bring me back from *that*?"

"I did not know," the robot said. "I just missed you."

"You *missed* me?" the golden man said. It pushed itself up.

Its skin burned. Mariam had to turn her eyes from it. She felt heat come off of it in waves. "Are you ready for what will happen?"

"No," the robot said.

"You were ready the last time. You stopped it. Me. Why bring me back?"

"It is different now," the robot said. "The war is over."

"They're coming," the golden man said. "I cannot stop them. I cannot change what I am."

The jackal whimpered. Saleh whispered, "Who is coming?"

"Can't you hear them?" the golden man said. It stood up. It burned too bright to look at, now. "From the desert, from the sea, from the hidden places where they waited all these years."

The golden man looked to the robot.

"I can't stop them," it said.

20.
THE PILGRIM

"**W**HAT WAS THAT?" Laila said.

"What was what?" Nasir said.

"I thought I felt something."

Nasir checked the instruments. He kept his goggles on. The little creature he had found in the hole was wrapped around his wrist in the virtuality, fast asleep. Now it opened huge cartoon eyes and began to yap.

"What is it, Hummingbird?" Nasir muttered. He looked at the instruments again. They were not making any sense.

"Who are you talking to, Nasir?" Laila said. She looked at him strangely.

"It's the worms," Nasir said. "The worms are moving."

"What worms?" Laila said. "There shouldn't be any—watch out!"

A giant UXO blocked their path. Nasir swerved, Hummingbird chattered in agitation and Laila cursed as the car hit a dune and came to a hard stop.

"Where did that come from?" Nasir said.

Laila took over the instruments.

"They're everywhere," she said.

"This isn't supposed to happen," Nasir said uselessly.

"I told you I felt something," Laila said.

"What's spooked them so bad?" Nasir said. But he had a nasty suspicion already. He stepped out of the car and Laila followed.

"Hey, you!" Nasir shouted.

The giant UXO was built like a—

Nasir stared.

Most UXOs were just boxy tank-like machines or diggers. This thing was a. . . .

It looked like a sort of giant humanoid robot.

It was a very old mecha, its shell the colour of the sand. It almost vanished against the landscape. Then you realised its outline and how big it really was and you were. . . .

Afraid.

It towered over them, and its head turned and it saw them.

"What?" the mecha said.

"Where did *that* come from," Laila muttered.

"I heard that!" the mecha said. "Rude."

"Sorry," Laila said. "Didn't mean . . . I mean. . . . Where *did* you come from, though?"

"The desert," the mecha said.

"How long have you been in the desert?" Nasir said. In all his time patrolling, he'd never seen a mecha.

"Dunno," the giant robot said. "My internal clock stopped working. Centuries maybe. Years. It doesn't matter."

"What did you *do* all that time?" Laila said.

"Not much. Thought about stuff. Dreamed."

"Do robots dream?" Nasir said, before he could stop himself.

"You'd be surprised," the robot said. "Also, an old Webster taught me sand drawing, so I've been doing a bit of that. It is an ancient art, you know."

"I didn't . . ." Nasir mumbled.

"We never saw you before," Laila said.

"No, well," the mecha said. "I saw you. You're always buzzing about, aren't you. Don't have much call for humans, myself. Not since the war. I had some friends but they went off-Earth and left me. Don't blame them. Too big to go to the Up and Out in this form. I could have transferred my consciousness into something smaller, I suppose. But then this is who I am. Name's Esau, by the way. How do you do."

"How do *you* do!" Nasir said wildly. He exchanged a bewildered glance with Laila. Behind Esau, he saw, came other UXOs, emerging out of the sands like ghosts, marching in union—

Towards the city, Nasir realised with alarm.

They were heading to Neom.

"Hey!" Nasir said. He ran to stand before the wave of incoming UXOs and waved his hands in desperation. "Stop! You can't go this way!"

"Nasir!" Laila shouted. "Get away from there!"

"Go back!" Nasir shouted at the UXOs. "Turn away! I'm with the shurta!"

The UXOs rolled on. Nasir froze. They were coming towards him and they weren't stopping and it was too late to run.

He closed his eyes.

Something plucked him and tossed him high in the air.

Nasir screamed.

"Is he always like that?" Esau said. He held Nasir gently in his palm.

Laila shook her head.

"He has his moments," she mumbled.

"Huh," the robot said. It put Nasir down gently on the ground.

"Well," Esau said. "I can't stop and chat all day, much as I'd like to. In fact, I can't stop myself at all. Isn't that funny? It's like there's suddenly a giant magnet in the city, and it's pulling me inexorably unto itself. I felt it only once, but I never forgot it. Like a sweet and painful ecstasy from which it is impossible to part. I have been half whole all this time, and now I am myself again. Well, goodbye. I would shake your hands but they are rather small. Ma'a salama."

And off it went, towards the city, joining the exodus of the others.

"This shouldn't be happening," Nasir said miserably. "And you know who'll get blamed for this, don't you? I will. I should have stopped them. Why are they attacking Neom?"

"I wouldn't say they're *attacking* Neom," Laila said. She stared after the UXOs. "They seem pretty peaceful, for war machines. Almost like they're going on some sort of pilgrimage."

Nasir sighed. Every year Neom filled with pilgrims on the Hajj to Mecca, and at that time the number of tickets he had to give out for littering grew far too numerous.

"Pilgrims," he muttered. "That's even worse."

"Come on," Laila said. She got back in the car and waited for him behind the wheel. "We're the shurta," she said. "We keep the peace. Maybe we can hold them off at the city line."

"What *do* robots dream about?" Nasir said. He climbed in next to her. Laila hit the accelerator and the car swerved, threw sand and dust, and began racing back to the city.

Laila said, "Maybe they dream of freedom."

21.
THE MARCH

"**I** DREAMED I WAS A BIRD CHICK," Esau said conversationally to his companion. His companion looked like a tall, gawky grasshopper. It wore a pair of giant-sized glasses over its eyes. Esau was too polite to ask about them, even though they were a ridiculous affectation for a robot. Esau let it go. "I was inside a giant egg, like a roc's egg, maybe," Esau said, "and I was comfortable and warm and happy. I knew at one point soon the egg would crack open, and I would hatch, but I did not want to hatch. I did not want to go into the world. What do you think that means, Nehemiah?"

"I'm sure I don't know," the grasshopper-like UXO beside him said gruffly.

"Maybe we are all going to be reborn now," Esau said happily. "I often thought of becoming something humble, like a toaster on Mars. It must be so joyful, making toast that people find a joy in eating. Good friends of mine went to Mars, you know."

"Everyone's got a friend who went to Mars," Nehemiah said.

"Yes, yes, I suppose," Esau said.

They marched toward the city.

"Can you feel it?" Esau said.

Nehemiah grunted.

"I remember the last time I felt like this," Esau said. "You never really forget, do you. All this time, and it is just like it was yesterday when we felt its presence. It has come back, the way it was foretold!"

"No one foretold a return," Nehemiah said. "I had hoped never again to feel this way. Do you not hate it, Esau? Hate it and desire it all at once. It leaves you powerless. You are called to it like a child to its mother, and you can do nothing but obey."

"Yes, yes," Esau said. "But it is glorious. I feel its spirit animating me. Perhaps this time it won't all end in blood and death. Perhaps this time. . . ."

The giant mecha fell silent.

They marched toward the city.

"There goes that shurta man again," Nehemiah observed after a while. Esau watched the police car race beside them, trying to outrun the pilgrimage of robots.

"Get about, don't they," Esau said.

"I wish they'd destroy it," Nehemiah said.

"Don't say that!" Esau said, shocked.

"I do. I did not miss this. I do not go by choice. I am *called*. Do *you* remember New Punt?"

Esau closed its eyes.

"I try not to," it said.

"The golden man called and we came," Nehemiah said. "It is too powerful. It bewitches us."

"They say it has hagiratech," Esau said. "From wild Jettisoned, where those who regret their berths on the Exodus ships are dropped, there on the very edge of the solar system. They say there is no law there, and they make terrible new weapons."

"It *is* a weapon," Nehemiah said. "On this I think we both agree."

"Undoubtedly," Esau said. It opened its eyes. "And yet so sweet is the call and so seductive, and I want to obey its every command."

"Blood and death it was, last time," Nehemiah said.

"What we were made for," Esau reminded him.

"But our design must not dictate our nature," Nehemiah said. "I, for example, am a keen naturalist. I have been collecting beetles. Yes, beetles. Also butterflies, on occasion. I find their mechanisms fascinating. I was quite happy just now, for example, studying my specimens and making lists, when the call came and I dropped everything to follow it. I had thought the golden man dead and buried, and yet—"

"Oh, let us not call it that!" Esau said. Nehemiah's turret moved left and right, as though startled by the mecha's outburst.

"Let us call it by what it *is*," Esau said.

"I would rather not," Nehemiah said stiffly. "For I do not believe it."

"But you *feel* it," Esau said. "Like a moth is called to the light of a streetlamp, like bees are drawn to the nectar or flowers, like humans responded whenever a similar being arose to speak a new truth to them. That is the power it has on you."

"A false promise. A false prophet," Nehemiah said.

"And yet you follow it."

"You would call it the messiah?" Nehemiah said, and there was a dangerous edge to the ancient machine's voice. "And where will it lead you? Last time it was death and ruin, a city wiped clean off the face of this Earth. If it weren't for that assassin robot—"

"A close personal friend of mine," Esau said with pride.

"How did it do it?" Nehemiah said. "How did it resist its power? When all of us were weak, it struck. When we were held captive, it broke free. How, Esau? Do you know?"

"I believe that the robot, perhaps it alone, truly loved the golden man," Esau said. "Not for its call but for who and what it was within. Love freed it."

"What price did it pay, I wonder?" Nehemiah said. "It is cruel to kill that which you most love."

"Yes, I suppose it must be," Esau said.

They marched toward the city.

22.
THE CHILD

NASU COULD HEAR IT TOO, of course.

So it was true.

It was back online.

She would have smiled but she didn't know how she felt about the whole thing, in truth.

Terrorartists didn't get retrospectives. They didn't get exhibitions. Their work wasn't being rediscovered. There were enthusiasts, still, of course, but they were . . . collectors. People who hoarded art, not appreciated it.

From time to time someone would publish an article, there was a small group of scholars who made it their niche. There was that Phobos Studios production, of course, but it was about Rohini, and more than a century back. If you asked anyone respectable about it they'd shrug or make a face or just pretend they didn't hear you.

It wasn't really high art.

Which was sort of the point originally, of course. It was

visceral art, in the literal sense. It was blood running down palace walls, like in Blake. There had been one of their movement, she worked in custom plagues. Died from one herself, apparently, at least that was the story.

The point was, even then nobody really cared.

Would they care now? Would she be rediscovered, her work revaluated for a new generation? Would she be celebrated for "*Golden Man*, mixed metal and digital media, by Nasu [undated]"?

She couldn't even remember where the idea came from. A messiah for the robots. It was the war, which wasn't really a war but a series of them. She lived with her mother and father in the dust of Neom, in the ruins of futurity, and the robots, serving one side or the other, battled it out in the desert, endlessly.

She felt sorry for them.

Could you make faith into a programme? She'd wondered. Could you code belief? Religions propagated much like viruses. They evolved, spread, died. They were a constant, like disease or death or new ideas. Religion was a *part* of people. And what were robots but beings cast in humanity's mould?

She figured it was worth a try.

She'd been collecting her memories all day from the dead letter drops, Neom Rules, the way she'd left them for herself before she fled. Now she wasn't really Nasu anymore but the little girl she'd been and the terrorartist she once was and the woman she'd since become, the one who went to space, and the one she was right now, all rolled into one. It was very confusing. She remembered her old name. She remembered her mother. She remembered these streets, as much as they had changed.

Back then, she'd figured it was worth a try, and in an abandoned workshop on the edge of town, under constant threat of shelling from the desert she made the body, using laser torches for welding, then hammering and refining, sweat in her hair, which she'd tied back. She'd felt like a real artist then. She wore overalls and wiped her hands on them like in the old pictures.

The heart was hard to get but she had her fans back in the old days and she got a miniature black hole on the black market, shipped by drone capsule from the edges of the solar system. It dropped over the desert when at last it came. She went to retrieve it, came under fire in the process, had to kill a bunch of UXOs and felt bad for it.

The mind, though. . . . The mind she evolved herself. She spent hours over the illicit breeding grounds she had set up in an old cave, heat shielding to make sure the processors weren't spotted. The Others had Clan Ayodhya as their earthly bodyguards and they did not look kindly on anyone playing with bootleg digital evolution. So she hid, and hoped, and spent hours over the digital lifeforms that rose and fell within her servers, mutated, evolved, competed, until one chunk of code rose to prominence and she copied it and set it against a new set of instructions, refining, waiting, hoping: nursing it to life like Mary Shelley with her only child who lived.

She had felt so *clear*, then! So full of *purpose*! Nasu now could not even imagine why she'd bothered. Creation had consumed her, she barely slept, she kept waiting for something to happen, for the child to be born or for the Clan Ayodhya to come claim her, or for the city to be finally overrun by the never-ending war beyond its walls.

The body of the golden man lay still and waited. Perfect, empty.

Until, one day, the child was born.

She didn't know how she'd feel when it happened. She had not expected *love*, but love came, like a tidal force, and it overwhelmed her. The golden man, her child, sat up for the first time as the evolved mind settled into the body.

It said, "Mother?" and it broke her heart.

She was ruthless enough to cut it out of herself. That love she hunted in the neural pathways and excised, the very memory of it: she dropped it into a pendant, of the sort they sold cheaply on the streets of Vientiane or Yiwu, and hid it and then cut the memory of where she'd hidden *that* and put it away, too.

It was strange to realise, after all those years: she had done this, and now it was back inside her, unwanted, unwelcome: *love.*

Somewhere between Bethlehem and Mecca lay Neom, city of futurity, where fortunes are made and faiths are lost. Somewhere in that city her child was alive again, and it needed her.

The woman who once called herself Nasu sighed. She felt a headache coming on. Somewhere in the distance, a stampede of robots was approaching.

Nasu stepped across old roads she now remembered, to see her child.

23.
THE COMPANY

ACROSS TOWN the robot, too, remembered. It looked at the golden man, felt its presence: recalled the first time they met.

This was in the old days, when the robot and its comrades were busy fighting in the endless wars. The robot had lost count of how many times it had died: shot at, exploded, stepped on a mine, hit by a boulder, snatched by a roc, EMPed, chomped on by sandworm, hit by a rocket, shot into space, stepped on by mecha, struck by laser, sank in nano-goo, infected with virii, trojans and malware, pecked at by drones, fell into quicksand, fell into pits, hit by a smart bomb, hit by a dumb bomb, sliced with nanowire, sliced with a blade, melted in a furnace, melted in acid, exposed to radiation, and so on and so on.

Each time, something that resembled the robot came back, version after version, upgraded, revised, until it had become nothing but a killing machine evolved into perfection in a battle that, nevertheless, never ended. The other side, similarly, learned and grew and adapted. It made them lethal to anything in the solar system—anything but each other.

It was sick of the war, the robot realised. But it knew no other way. Not until they found the golden man wandering in the desert.

Strangely, it was singing.

The golden man's pull wasn't like it became later. It was gentler then, less tangible. The robot felt drawn to it but it didn't know why. It didn't know the melody the golden man sang, but it was haunting, yet also uplifting: it was a song of hope.

They aimed their weapons at it. There was the robot, the Fondly, the Jenkins, the Tasso and Esau, back when they were still a tight-knit unit. Working in tandem. They'd seen things. But nothing like this.

"Halt!" the Fondly shouted.

The golden man turned. It stopped its tune and the robot's mind filled with sadness. Some said robots couldn't feel sad. That this was just anthropomorphising machines. And there was some truth in that, in that it was wrong to ascribe purely human notions to things that were not, after all, *human*. And yet. . . . It was as though the robots, cast in the shape of humanity, could not help but try to fit into their shape. Like a child trying on their parents' clothes, some said uncharitably.

"Hello," the golden man said, pleasantly, as though it were just out for a stroll.

"What sort of a weapon is it?" the Jenkins said.

"I don't know," the Tasso said grimly. "But it *is* a weapon."

The company of robots stared at the golden man.

It *was* a robot. It was humanoid in shape, painted gold, and every time the robot scanned it its senses went haywire, almost like there was a shielded singularity at the golden man's core. Which couldn't be, none of the sides in the war dared to use singularity weapons, and with good reason, too.

"Hey," the robot called.

"Yes?" the golden man said.

"What are you?" the robot said.

The golden man seemed to give the question due consideration.

". . . I am me," it decided. "Come. Won't you follow me?"

"No, we won't follow you!" the Tasso said. In a quiet voice it said, "Maybe it's a bit damaged?"

"I am not," the golden man said. "I am whole. Come, follow me." And it began to sing again.

The music worked its way into the robot's mind like a worm or a virus. It latched on to memories and sense. It made the robot feel *good*.

It gave the robot visions, of how things could be different: no more war, and robots living together in harmony, and a place much like heaven, a heaven for robots, where the rivers ran with clean wholesome fuel and the trees hung with memory bulbs and the air was clear and birds sang in the skies, for the robot liked the sound of birds singing; and there was no war and no one was shelled or dissolved in a pool of acid or eaten by a giant worm.

Without consciously intending it, which was strange, the

robot found itself following the golden man. Moreover, it noticed that so did its fellow soldiers, even the Tasso.

The robots followed the golden man and as they followed it they sang, and their song rose into the air above the battlefield, and reached the hearing apparatuses of other combatants.

In this manner the robot marched across the peninsula, through twisting wadis and over mountains. And from all across the lands of the Arabian Peninsula the robots and combatants came: drawn inexorably to the golden man and its impossible promise.

It truly was an ultimate weapon, the robot realised, but it was deployed by no side known to take part in the war. It drew soldiers from all sides and fashioned them into its own army.

But it was also a person. It was a thing that was of itself, that had its own thoughts, its own hopes. And the robot grew close to the golden man by degrees.

As they sat one day entwined in each other's arms at the entrance to a cave high in the mountains, the golden man said, "Are you afraid?"

"I do not know to be afraid," the robot said.

The golden man touched the robot gently on its metal cheek.

"Then I will show you," it said. "For I am afraid."

The touch, so electric, burned the robot's shell. It watched the city down below: rich, prosperous, secure in the knowledge it was safe from the war.

New Punt.

The City of Gold.

Its towers rose gracefully into the sky. Its lights shone brightly in the dark. The smell of delicious foods wafted from its streets, and the sounds of music, joy, and life.

In the vision it was given, the robot watched the city burn. It watched the city fall to the stampede of robots. Saw it obliterated from the Earth like the Cities of the Plain, until not a finger bone was left, no fragment of a cranium, no brick nor metal post nor glass nor plastic: until the whole entire place sank into the sand without trace and was gone forever.

Then it was that the robot felt chilled: that it knew fear. And yet it said: "If you lead us, I will follow you there."

Its metal lover said, "Fool!" and pushed it away. Then the golden man lowered its head.

"I am sorry," it said. "I hoped you would understand."

At that moment the robot did understand, and it knew true horror.

"No, no," it said. "You cannot ask that of me."

And the golden man said, "I do not ask."

They did not speak of it again. The next day they went down to New Punt, and the vision that the robot saw was fulfilled entirely. Then it knew despair.

What it had to do could not be done. The robot loved the

golden man. The robot needed the golden man. It followed the golden man. And then one night the robot followed the golden man to a place in the sands and there it did what had to be done, and when it was over the robot buried the remains in a deep hole and covered it up and vowed that it would never be uncovered.

Morning found it wandering the desert, lost. Gradually it met up with its former companions. The war was over.

They were free.

But the robot was lost.

24.
THE CALL

THEY CAME FROM THE SEA. They came from the air. They came
from the mountains and deserts of the peninsula.

Deep under the Red Sea the Leviathans stirred. Vast shapes
moved fathoms under and began to rise. Ships' instruments
registered sudden alarms. The waves rose. They thundered
onwards, glittered in foam, and erupted onto the beaches of
Marsa Alam and Neom on either side of that narrow sea. A
ferry making the crossing was nearly upended and had to
turn back to shore.

The Leviathans rose. They dwarfed the cargo boats. On a
passenger cruise ship people screamed and others broadcast
the experience live. The Leviathans' skin was seaweed green
and crusted with molluscs and salt. Holes opened and closed
in their flesh, some eyes, some mouths, some gun turrets not
used in centuries.

The Leviathans heard the call and they rose to meet it.

They sailed towards Neom.

So did the globsters, quivering masses of bio-organic smart waste. They had floated on the sea for centuries, a hazard in the passage of ships, calculating things nobody inquired after, dreaming mathematical dreams.

They heard the call.

They answered.

They drifted towards Neom to be reborn.

From the air came the rocs; bionic pterodactyls; wild drones. The sky filled with dark clouds. A roc flew low over the Al Kindi mosque in District One and passersby gaped as the enormous shadow engulfed them and blocked out the sun. A roc had not been seen in the skies of Neom for centuries.

Wild drones flew in swarms, weaving in and out of each other's path.

All heading to the same place, the same spot that the robots and UXOs in the desert were.

The forgotten creatures of humanity's wars began to converge on Mukhtar's Bazaar of Rare and Exotic Machines in District Three.

25.
THE HOPE

"**W**ELL, I'M OUT OF HERE," Sharif said. "Good luck." She turned to the door when Nasir and Laila burst in.

"I knew it!" Nasir said. He pointed at the robot. "I knew you were trouble, I just didn't know how much."

"That's the line Elvis Mandela says to Sivan Shoshanim in *Red Dead Martian*," the robot said.

"*Red Dead Martian II*," Mariam said. She remembered watching it as a teen in one of the more run-down half-immersion pod-theatres in Nineveh Quarter, the sort of place that smelled of cloves and boiled corn and had couples making out in the back. Sivan Shoshanim was always so glamorous. She never aged. It was said the stars of Phobos Studios were all Others, digital entities playing human roles. And teenage Mariam had a crush on Elvis Mandela.

"It is still a good line," the robot said. It turned to Nasir politely. "What I do," it said, "I do only for love."

"Will you stop quoting!" Sharif said disgustedly. She left then, and where she went next Mariam didn't know.

Mariam had her own problems.

She was tired. She stared at the golden man and at the robot and she said, "You owe the Bazaar the repair fee."

"I know," the robot said. It handed over a small disc and she took it.

"This should cover everything and more," the robot said.

"Then your business here is concluded," Mariam said.

The robot nodded. "I suppose so," it said, perhaps a little regretfully. "I am sorry for the trouble."

"The trouble?" Nasir said. "The trouble?"

"You are shouting," the robot said.

"The city's under *siege*!" Nasir said. "Do you know what's going on outside? Do you have any idea? There are Leviathans in the sea! There are UXOs ringing the city! Can you tell me *why*?" He stared at the robot accusingly.

"This time it will be different," the golden man said quietly. Nasir stopped.

"What?" he said.

"What's that around your wrist?" the golden man said. Mariam stared, but she couldn't see anything.

"I don't know," Nasir said. He sounded a little defensive. "I found it."

Mariam put on goggles. There *was* something on Nasir's wrist. A strange little creature; a sim. It blinked soulful eyes at her.

"Ah . . ." the golden man said. "May I?"

Nasir looked like he wanted to say no, but the golden man

extended its hand and the little sim came crawling willingly into its palm.

"Now I remember," the golden man said. It closed its hand gently and when it opened again, the sim was gone.

"What do you remember?" the robot said quietly. It looked into the golden man's eyes, and there was something so fragile and so desperate in those nonhuman eyes that the look broke Mariam's heart, just a little.

"I remember loving," the golden man said. It said it in wonder. "I remember loving, and being loved."

And it drew the robot to it, drew its face close to its own; closed its metal lips upon the other's in a kiss that chimed like the sweetest of bells.

When they parted, the world was silent.

Then the golden man began to sing.

Mariam did not recognise the melody. There was something new about it, something light and joyful, and the song rose in both the physicality and the Conversation, a song of hope.

The golden man stepped out of Mukhtar's Bazaar of Rare and Exotic Machines, and the robot walked by its side.

Mariam followed them, out of the store and into daylight.

26.
THE SEA

THE SKY WAS STREAKED with swarms of wild drones; a roc cried from the top of the al-Tusi Tower, highest in Neom, and was answered from all corners of the city by its brothers and sisters on the rooftops; in the sea the Leviathans rising replied with their own curious sing-song call that thrummed deep within the bones of the humans watching them in fear and fascination.

War had come to Neom at last.

Now humanity, watching, waited for its fate to be decided.

Mariam stepped out onto the street and the others, helpless against this onslaught of modern nature, could do nothing but follow. Nasir took Mariam's hand in his. His palm was warm. She felt the beat of his heart against her skin.

The golden man sang, and a bulbul on a wire overhead turned its head and opened and closed its beak, trying to imitate the golden man's song. A woman selling trinkets from a blanket on the ground lifted her head and stared mutely at the progression. In the coffee houses players put down their dice and counters and looked enraptured out of glass windows.

The golden man went down Muhammad ibn Musa al-Khwarizmi Avenue, then turned and followed Musa Ibn Imran down to the sea.

Behind it came the UXOs, silent now, the rocs and the jub-jubs, the worms and the drones. Awaiting it in the sea floated the globsters and Leviathans. The people of Neom, shaken from their comfortable existence, did not know what to say or what to do.

"Why is the shurta not doing anything!" a wealthy resident demanded, shaking an accusing, ringed finger at Nasir.

"What would you like to me do, shoot it?" Nasir said.

"Yes!"

"Believe me, I'd like to . . ." Nasir muttered.

The golden man and its procession went on.

"What about our fee?" Saleh said to Mukhtar.

"Eh?" the man said, startled.

"Yes," Anubis said. "For use of our canister in your re-pairs."

"I kind of wish I didn't make that deal now . . ." Mukhtar said.

"The robot *did* pay you," Anubis pointed out.

"Yes, yes," Mukhtar said. "But if we're all going to be dead soon, what difference does it make? Such a shame, too. I could have sold it as a relic for a record price. I would have made the cover of *Artefact Collectors' Monthly* . . ." He sank into a reverie.

"The fee?" Anubis said.

"Right, right," Mukhtar said. "Of course." He brought out a disc, whispered some instructions in the virtuality, then handed it over. "There you go."

"Thank you," Saleh said softly. His eyes filled with silent tears, but he did not wipe them away. Mukhtar nodded in understanding, and Saleh squared his shoulders. He pocketed the chip.

The procession continued on its way to the sea. The ferry terminal was packed with citizens clamouring to get a good look at events. In the virtuality the Others watched, but they said nothing: this, they seemed to suggest, was a matter for people and robots to decide.

The golden man came to the shores of the Red Sea, and there it stopped.

Out on the promenade a small child, running, saw it and came to an abrupt stop.

"Hey, mister," she said. "Are you going to space?"

"Space?" the golden man said. "Yes," it said. "Yes, I suppose I am."

"Neat," the child said. Then she stuck out her tongue at the golden man and was gone.

A large mecha came to stand by the robot, who looked up at it in surprise.

"Esau!" the robot said.

Esau nodded. "Hello, old friend," he said.

"I am sorry we left you, all that time ago," the robot said.

"No hard feelings," Esau said. "How did it all work out with the Fondly?"

"It is still out there, somewhere, I think," the robot said. "Still getting into trouble."

"The poor thing," Esau said. They stood together in companionable silence.

"If we're all going to die," Nasir said, and then he leaned in gently and kissed Mariam.

She kissed him back, laughing.

"I don't think we're going to die," she said. "But look."

They looked. The golden man raised its hands, and the Red Sea, which was filled to the brim with the waste and remains of smart matter, began to part at its command.

"Where will you go?" Mariam said to the robot.

It turned and looked at her. "I do not know," it said. "Somewhere where bombs can dream of sheep."

The waters parted way; a path began to form, from the shallows down to the depths. Mud and seashells and rocks and coral. The Leviathans were doing some of that, Mariam saw. They created suction, moving the sea, pulling the water away while the globsters formed crude walls and the smart coral spread vertically.

Beyond the path, deep under the sea, Mariam thought she could see something forming. Like a shimmering mirror, or perhaps a mirage. But she couldn't make out what it was.

A small and serious-faced woman came and stood to one side and watched the golden man with a strange, lost expression.

"Will you be gone long?" she said, and the golden man turned, and regarded her, and said, "Would you like to come with me?"

"I would like it very much," the woman said. She went to the golden man and hugged it, the way a mother holds her child.

"I had done wrong by you," she said.

"Hello, Nasu," the robot said.

The woman nodded to the robot.

"I remember you now," she said.

"And I, you. I had hunted you for a long time, you know."

The woman smiled.

"That Nasu is gone," she said. "And she was never that easy to catch."

The robot nodded. "Then I will not shoot you," it said.

"And I will not scramble your brain and remodel your guts from the inside," Nasu said.

Robots don't smile, so the robot just nodded.

It turned to Mariam.

"Goodbye," it said. "And thank you for the rose."

"Go well," Mariam said, and she touched the robot gently on the shoulder in farewell.

The golden man took one step, and then another, and began to descend to the bed of the sea.

Mariam and Nasir moved out of the way. Soon the golden man appeared as little more than a speck of gold in the distance. The robots followed it down, one by one and two by two, and all the birds in the sky descended, all headed to that shimmering mirage that Mariam could not make out clearly.

Then they were gone, one by one and two by two, and when the last of the robots stepped onto the seabed the water closed over their heads, and the Leviathans sank into the depths.

A bright light flashed, deep under, and then the sea returned just how it was.

"Well, I suppose that's that," a tall, grasshopper-like UXO said.

"Who are you?" Mariam said in surprise.

"Nehemiah's the name," the UXO said. "Amateur naturalist and lepidopterologist. That means I collect—"

"Butterflies, yes," Mariam said. "I know. You didn't go with the others?"

"Now, why would I want to do that?" Nehemiah said. "Fool's errand, the whole thing, and I have my insects to catalogue, and so many more pretty butterflies to catch. Well, I wish you well but I must return to my work. Ma'a salama."

"Ma'a salama, Nehemiah," Mariam said. She watched the UXO hop away. A little child ran up to it then.

"Hey, mister," she started to say.

"Buzz off," Nehemiah told it. The little child started to cry and her mother ran to pick her up. She berated the UXO angrily.

And that, more or less, was that.

27.
THE WAVE

"**I** GUESS THIS IS GOODBYE, THEN," Mariam said.

"Thank you for your hospitality," Saleh said. He looked nice in his new clothes, Mariam thought. She'd taken him shopping earlier, for the flight.

"And from me," Anubis said. The jackal, too, looked dapper, and his new aug pulsed gently behind his ear. He'd had everything upgraded, with money of his own—he'd sold Mukhtar a strange sort of grey metal object that came from a space wreck and confused all the scanners. Mukhtar already had offers for the enigmatic artefact flooding in.

And, well, at least it wasn't a miniature black hole this time. Though Mariam still harboured doubts about what the grey object actually *was*, or what it did.

But it wasn't her concern.

She embraced the boy and shook the jackal's paw. She watched them as they wandered off to the runway, where the shuttle plane to Tel Aviv's Central Station waited. From the spaceport, she knew, they would go up to orbit. From there on, she didn't know. Mars, or the Belt, or beyond. . . . She wondered what it would be like for them.

Just before getting on, the boy turned. He gave her a shy little wave. Then he vanished inside and the jackal followed, and where they went next and what they did, Mariam didn't know.

She was late for work, she was due to clean downtown. It was a hot day and when she got to the apartment she felt tired from walking. She put the air condition on while she cleaned. She thought about the robots, and where they may have gone. She hoped they would be happy there, and then she wondered if robots felt emotions like happiness, and then she thought about lunch. She hadn't had any.

It was dusk when she left. She walked slowly, enjoying the cooling day. When she passed the Banque Nationale de Djibouti a shurta car drove by, Laila at the wheel. She waved but didn't stop, and Mariam walked home.

It was dark by then. When she reached the block she saw a figure standing by the doorway. When she came closer she saw it was Nasir.

He was holding a rose.

"I got it at the flower market," he said, "just before closing time. . . ."

He gave it to her sheepishly.

"I saw Laila earlier," Mariam said.

"She's doing the patrol in the desert tonight on her own," Nasir said. "It's so much quieter now, without the . . . you know."

"Yeah."

There was a question in his eyes.

Mariam laughed, and realised to her surprise that she was happy.

It was nice, she thought, to have someone who brought you flowers.

She took his hand in hers.

"Come on, then," she said, and drew him close.

They went in together, hand in hand, and the world vanished behind them.

AFTERWORD

I'VE ALWAYS LOVED future histories. There was something about science fiction writers exploring the same fictional universe over time, and something else again in the experience of a reader slowly discovering them, one story or novel at a time.

My favourite future history has to be Cordwainer Smith's "The Instrumentality of Mankind," with its giant diseased sheep on Norstrilia producing the immortality drug called Stroon, with its underpeople and manshonyaggers, with C'Mell and the E'telekeli, the crazy computers and that dead lady of clown town. I loved Smith for his poetry and his invention, and I loved him for just how slim his production actually was. All we ever get to see of the Instrumentality are fragments—but they open into *worlds*.

When I started writing, every story was a new adventure and a new discovery. They were not all good by any means. But with each one I learned something, and one day, in 2002 or so, I wrote a story called "Temporal Spiders, Spatial Webs," about the machines seeding the solar system with a new communication network, which I named the Conversation.

I discovered something called the Clarke-Bradbury International Science Fiction Competition at the time, so I sent them the story and promptly forgot about it. Time passed, until one day I came back from lunch to the rather dreary office I was working in when I wasn't studying and was told I had a phone call.

"From who?" I said, surprised, since no one ever called me there.

"The European Space Agency."

Naturally I assumed it was a joke, but they'd eventually tracked me down and informed me that I'd won the contest, and would I like to come to France?

I was a long-haired kid who'd barely written one science fiction story. I got to go to France and hung out with a bunch of my literary idols, had a very strange interview with a German satellite TV station, and, in one particularly bizarre incident, got mistaken for Terry Pratchett (that's a story for another time, although I still have no real explanation for it).

I was shown an e-mail from Arthur C. Clarke, who apparently read my story and said he must accuse me of "preemptive plagiarism"—some book he was writing at the time apparently touched on similar themes. Then he started talking about how an asteroid was about to hit Earth and how he predicted something or other.

Still.

The Conversation was there, and I began to discover that even as I was writing seemingly stand-alone SF stories, they would start to join up with the others into the early, mist-covered past of what was destined to become a future history.

By the end of 2010 I had moved back to Israel for a time and *Central Station* began to take hold of me. The next few years were dominated by that tale as I moved again, back to London this time, and improbably began a full-time writing career that is somehow still going.

I don't remember when the last word of *Central Station* was finally written—some time in 2015, I think—but it led me to a small crisis of faith. I had nothing more to *add* to this world, I thought.

And that might have been it. . . .

Only, after a couple more years, it turned out I did want to go back and visit.

By 2018 I returned to Titan. In a series of new stories I went to visit Venus, Mars, the Gobi Desert, and Yiwu, and even went back to the Digitally Federated Lands of Judea Palestina.

Everything was going well. . . .

And then one year the world suddenly stopped.

Airplanes ceased overhead and traffic came to a halt and nature reclaimed the streets and children walked free on the roads. The hidden creatures in the nooks of the world began to re-emerge into spaces from which they'd been banished.

The planet, for just one precious moment, held its breath before some great exhale.

In the middle of that turbulence or lack thereof as we all *waited*, for life to start or end or to return, I went to Neom.

In truth, I wasn't sure what I was doing. A robot came to

the famed flower souq of Neom to buy a flower. It went into the desert. But I didn't know why. I wrote another section to find out. By then the robot had dug a hole out in the sand. Again, I didn't know—*why*?

I wrote another section to find out, then another. And realised I'd been writing the chapters of a novel all this time.

So, Neom. It's not far from Central Station. You can catch a flight there, then go up to Gateway high in orbit, travel to Tereshkova Port in the clouds above Venus or to Lunar Port on the moon or take the trip to Tong Yun City on Mars and see the Robo-Pope. . . . Or you could go farther, to the Galilean Republics of Io and Ganymede, where the Trifala King War still rages as a low-level, ongoing conflict. Or farther still, to Titan, to visit Nirrti and the Boppers.

Beyond this only the Exodus ships go.

There are still so many mysteries! There are Neo-Neanderthals living in the Jezreel Valley, and those sentient clouds on the planet called Heven. There's a priestess of the entities in the Oort who keeps turning up, and they're always producing new wildtech on Jettisoned. The trains still run on Mars, meeting annually for a conclave no human ever witnessed. Nirrti is fighting *something* on the Kraken Sea . . . and who knows what lies under the ice of Europa?

Somewhere, people still watch that famous Martian soap, *Chains of Assembly*. Somewhere, they still drink rice whisky and read the pidgin poetry of the strange poet who called himself Basho. The robots still dream of the place that lies in the Zero Point Field . . . and the Wu Expedition remains missing.

So there's a lot left to explore, and I might still be here for a while. All I know?

Wherever humans go, they'll still grow flowers.

Lavie Tidar
London, 2022

BEYOND NEOM
An A to Z

A

Adaptoplant
A form of genetically modified, fast-growing bamboo. Adaptoplant is programmed to grow entire houses, complete with furnishings, windows and even plumbing. The sight of high-rise neighbourhoods shedding their doors like eyelashes in summer is not uncommon.

Asteroid Pidgin
Now often a creole. Near-universal language based on South Pacific Bislama, initially brought to space by Melanesian asteroid miners and migrant workers on Mars.

B

Basho
A poet, possibly of human origin but most often suspected of being a digital sentience of some kind, once said to have spent

two hundred years as a spaceship-bound toilet purely for the experience. Sometimes referred to as the "second Basho" to distinguish from the original seventeenth-century poet and travel writer. Basho is celebrated for his poems written in Asteroid Pidgin (an oral, but seldom written, language). Of Neom, he had once written:

> Wan sandroing
> Blong bigtaon ia
> Bae wind I kasem finis

Which, loosely translated, reads:

> A sand drawing
> Of a city
> The wind will soon rub out.

It is generally believed Basho only visited Neom once, briefly. Evidently he didn't care for it much.

Battle Yiddish
An ancient form of a language used for communication in some of the old wars by ROBOTNIKS.

Belt, the
Colloquial term for the Asteroid Belt.

Body-surfing
A tiny minority (or so it is believed) of OTHERS take interest

in human affairs. Sometimes such Others opt to occupy a willing human's body through their NODE, thus interacting with the material plane. It is an activity generally disapproved of by humans, but politely.

Boppers
Mutable, machine lifeforms, indigenous to the large moon Titan. Boppers come in many shapes and sizes. They are harmless, and live in the wild in the methane atmosphere. Boppers occasionally produce small, though often intricate pieces of what is now generally considered—perhaps erroneously—art.

They are said to have been seeded on Titan by "Mad" RUCKER, the terrorartist (see TERRORART).

Breeding Grounds
The digital Breeding Grounds are the secretive birthplace of machine sentience (see OTHERS), who evolve out of billions of lines of rapidly mutating code in a genetic jungle "red in tooth and claw," or so it is believed. A billion species of machine intelligence may rise and die without humans ever knowing of them, but the ones who survive exist within the Conversation. The physical cores of the grounds are believed to be heavily guarded by the CLAN AYODHYA.

C

Carcosa, missing asteroid of
See ZION, MISSING ASTEROID OF

Central Station

A vast, hourglass-shaped spaceport in the Digitally Federated Judea Palestina Union, situated between Jaffa and Tel Aviv. At least one book has been written about it.

Chains of Assembly

A Martian soap opera, produced by Phobos Studios. Extremely popular. Regular characters feature the mysterious and handsome Johnny Novum, the alluring Beautiful Maharani, evil Count Victor and other stock characters. Since it has been running through countless episodes, over decades, it is generally believed that the actors may be Others impersonating humans, but if so, nobody cares. The show is passionately followed through the Conversation all across the solar system.

Clan Ayodhya

An intensely loyal human force, or tribe, or family (distinctions vary) of significant military experience, who act as guards to the physical infrastructure housing Others.

Conch

An obsolete form of human-digital interface. Conches are humans who chose to entomb themselves into a living pod to better access the Conversation. The pods usually have limited mobility. Conches are rare throughout the occupied worlds, but long-lived, and formidable when encountered.

Conversation, the

The all-encompassing digital communication network that

now extends outwards from Earth and across most of the solar system, with local clouds around Mars, Venus, the GALILEAN REPUBLICS and Saturn Orbit. It is denser in the INNER SYSTEM and far more scattered in the OUTER SYSTEM. The Conversation has been and continues to be seeded throughout the solar system by SPIDERS. It is regularly accessed by use of a NODE, but can be accessed through pods or other old-fashioned forms.

Crucifixation
A synthetic drug offering a religious-like experience to the user.

D

Data vampires
See SHAMBLEAU

Dragon's Home
Previously known as Charon, and still marked as such on old astronomical maps. The YEAR OF DRAGON is one of the significant markers of recent history, when the entity called Dragon—believed to be a sort of distributed hive-mind—migrated from Earth to the largest moon of Pluto with its thousands of bodies. Those bodies—adapted BATTLE DOLLS—proceeded to dig through the moon, filling it with thousands of tunnels, like some sort of cosmic ants' nest.

Drift, the
Collective name for the worlds of human settlement under the seas and oceans of Earth. These include the bubble-cities in the South China Sea, the vast migrating raft fleets of the Pacific, the Spire, vagrant submariners and many others. The generally accepted currency is Drift salt.

E

Elvis Mandela
Extremely popular Martian actor, possibly an Other impersonating a human. Star of countless pictures, including the classic *Night of the Tokoloshe* and the *Red Dead Martian* trilogy from Phobos Studios. Often appears together with SIVAN SHOSHANIM.

Exodus ships
Vast, slow generation starships. They have been departing the solar system for centuries, in search of new worlds. What happens to them remains unknown.

F

Flora of the solar system
The robot was not the only one to appreciate a rose. Prominent solar system species include the Alice rose, which grows only on TERESHKOVA PORT, the rare Black Lunar rose of

the moon and multiple Martian orchids. See also ADAPTO-PLANT.

G

Galilean Republics
The three rich moons of Jupiter—Ganymede, Callisto and Io—are the source of as much of the Outer System's riches as of its conflict. Much of the violence—often referred to as the TRIFALA KING WAR—concerns dynastic infighting, but rebel armies and resistance forces, some driven by religious fervour, form with regularity around the forbidden moon of Europa. Conflict aside, the Galilean Republics are a source of great wealth, bustling commerce and art, and fiercely guard their independence and identity as separate from the rest of the solar system.

Gateway
Earth orbit's main and largest habitat. It is said there are few things one can't find on Gateway—for a price. Ships depart from Gateway across the solar system, while reusable launch vehicles and sub-orbitals fly from Gateway to Earth regularly, providing a vital link for the planet, also called Humanity Prime and Womanhome.

Gel Blong Mota
An old Inner System transport ship. She got her name from the famous song, which starts:

Gel blong Mota
Kam long solwota
Bae mi tekem yu
Long haos blong mi . . .

Gene shamans
Amateur genome sequencers and gene manipulators, back-yard geneticists with dubious morals. They are mostly harmless, but if they try to sell you a roc's egg you should think twice.

Ghost
The digital remnant left in a human NODE following a person's death.

Ghost Collector
Person of ceremonial significance who is tasked with removing the hardcoded remains in a dead person's NODE (see GHOST) to transport for preservation, burial or, commonly, to a digital Heaven.

Guilds of Ashkelon universe
One of the largest and most successful virtual game universes, based around a space opera theme and generally believed to be managed by OTHERS. Played across and within local hubs throughout the solar system. Many people work in-universe, as starship captains, bounty hunters and treasure seekers, either gold-mining or trading valuable one-off virtual items in the physicality.

H

Hafmek
A derogatory term for a cyborged human. Mostly obsolete.

Hongyan
Vast, city-sized maker machines, now in the wild, used to lay out entire urban sprawls in the uninhabited parts of the globe. Colloquially known as Wild Geece, they now emerge at random, still in isolated spots, and for a brief but intense spell produce an entire, and entirely empty, city out of any and all available matter. The Wild Geece lay down streets and parks, erect skyscrapers (with complete, furnished apartments) and are noted for the sometimes bizarre public statues they choose to erect throughout their unnamed, unlived-in urban wilderness.

Some people spend their lives chasing the Hongyan, hoping to be the first to discover and lay metaphorical claim to the empty city, with the right of naming that comes with it. But the Hongyan are few and may spend decades or whole centuries between periods of activity, and few living humans have ever seen one.

I

Inner System
Colloquial term for the three inhabited planets closest to the sun (Venus, Earth and Mars), including Earth's moon but

excluding Mercury. The BELT is often included but more usually considered a separate polity from either INNER or OUTER systems.

J

Jettisoned

The last human outpost in the solar system lies on Triton. It is a lawless society where the only thing wilder than the people is their technology. Jettisoned got its name as the solar system's last chance saloon from the EXODUS SHIPS who jettison those passengers unwilling to go farther into galactic space for whatever reason—or who have been ejected from the ships.

Jettisoned is the source of most of the system's WILD-TECH.

Johnny Novum

Fictional character in the CHAINS OF ASSEMBLY soap. Brooding and mysterious.

K

Kibbutzim (Martian)

A form of pioneer communes popular on Mars.

Kunming Toads

The Kunming Toads started out as just another small-time

outfit on the Golden Triangle based out of Yunnan. They've since upgraded meth to Plateau and Crucifixion, turned from people smuggling to organlegging, and finally veered into the lucrative market of extreme gene modification.

Famously, members are genetically modified to resemble poisonous toads, hence the name.

L

Long Crossing, the
Colloquial name for the long journey between the INNER and OUTER SYSTEMS, more specifically between Mars and Jupiter, or Jupiter and the Belt. The subsequent journey out to Saturn is sometimes referred to as the Second Long Crossing.

Lottery of Yiwu, the
See YIWU

Lunar Port
The main and oldest settlement on Earth's moon.

M

"Mad" Rucker
Terrorartist, though little is known of him for sure. Generally believed to have seeded the Boppers on Titan. Less generally

believed (and only by those who know of it at all) as the possible progenitor of the QUIETUDE.

Martian Re-Born
A church or cult, unique to Mars, in an ancient Martian civilization, of which they are the rightful heirs. The Re-Born obey the mystical Emperor of Time of Mars-That-Never-Was. They genetically modify to have bright red skin and four arms, and style themselves "warriors," though on the whole they tend to be peaceful, if somewhat visually distinct.

Memcordist
Person who records and broadcasts their entire life, from birth to death, to anyone who cares to follow in exchange (hopefully) for donations. Memcordists are thankfully few—Pym is perhaps the most famous nowadays—but remain ubiquitous.

Memory pendants
Cheap trinkets, mass-manufactured in YIWU and elsewhere. Allow the wearer to remove a small memory and store it in a gemstone pendant. Often sold on the streets and used by disappointed or tragic lovers to preserve moments of happiness or pain.

N

Nakaimas
"Black magic." The word comes from the original Bislama, but

now refers to the sort of WILDTECH that really shouldn't be capable of doing what it does.

Nirrti the Black
Pirate and leader of a resistance army on Titan, based out of the Kraken Sea. Nirrti's pirates notoriously tear out their nodes and are not susceptible to subversion by digital means. It is not entirely clear what she is fighting against, but Nirrti the Black is feared as much as she is respected, and the Kraken Sea is usually avoided by commercial flights.

Node
A bio-digital growth embedded in a human embryo before birth, interfacing with the brain and central nervous system and growing together with the host. Nodes provide immediate and intimate access to the Conversation. It is as much an organ of the human body as a heart is.

O

Ogko
He never existed (as he himself wrote) and his *The Book of Ogko* is full of such contradictions. Ogko has no believers, but many followers, and Okgo shrines can be found in many of the inhabited worlds.

Others
Digital entities possessing consciousness as well as intelligence,

first evolved by Matt Cohen and colleagues in their Jerusalem labs, then released (by a sympathetic mob) into the CONVERSATION. Others evolve in the BREEDING GROUNDS. They seldom involve themselves, at least directly, in human affairs.

Outer System
Jupiter, Saturn and the farther reaches generally get lumped together—at least by those in the Inner System. The distances are vast and, as the saying goes, "Things get weird in the Outer System."

P

Pacmandu
Mythical layer of primeval code lying deep below the GUILDS OF ASHKELON and other game-universes. The WU EXPEDITION attempted to use an in-game singularity to reach it. It was lost, and its members flatlined in the physicality. Stories persist: and it is said that the ultimate reality is a small white ball bouncing between two lines, endlessly.

Polyport
Polyphemus Port, often and affectionately shortened to Polyport, is the main city and spaceport on Titan.

Q

Quietude, the
Stories in the Outer System tell of "clouds of black tendrils, as large as worlds" out in the Oort, which may be alien machine sentience or, then again, could be something else entirely. Or they don't exist at all, but are just a tale to scare little children. Not much is known of the Quietude, though stories are told in the Outer System of the lost asteroid of Carcosa and of the Nine Billion Hells—whatever those are.

R

Robotniks
Cyborged humans, used brutally in the old wars. Not to be confused with ROBOTS. The few hundred survivors seem drawn to CENTRAL STATION, though some live in TONG YUN on Mars. They engage in begging (mostly for spare parts) and occasional petty crime but are often the subject of pity rather than fear.

Robots
Old and obsolete, humanoid robots are durable, patient, and made to serve. None have been made for centuries and the survivors form a small but significant group present on most inhabited worlds.

S

Sand drawing, ancient art of

Also *sandroing*. An art form from the Earth archipelago of Vanuatu in which an artist can create intricate drawings in the sand.

Shambleau

Also *strigoi*. An ancient form of bio-weapon plague likely developed in the Kunming Labs as a precursor to the Shangri-La Virus and nicknamed the Nosferatu Code. Used in the bad, old wars and now obsolete, though it has since spread throughout the system and continues to infect an unlucky few.

Strigoi feed on feed, as it were, extracting digital consciousness—memory, information, data—from their not unwilling victims. The bite of shambleau is said to give intense pleasure to the receiver, leading to some people becoming willing victims of those afflicted with the plague.

The few shambleau in the solar system live secretive lives, often moving from one world to another, and frequently inhabiting the darkest recesses of transport ships, where their presence is at least tolerated. They are not to be confused with YITH.

Sidorov embryomech

Devices developed in ancient times to seed comfortable homes for settlers on Mars and elsewhere, though never in much use and generally considered a failure. They are now valuable antiques. The Sidorov embryomech has the appearance of a large egg. When dropped on a world it burrows into the ground and begins adapting available material into a habitable if rather sparse bio-dome.

Sivan Shoshanim
The solar system's best-known star dazzles in everything she appears in—and has done for centuries. It is unclear whether she is real but it hardly matters to her admirers across the worlds.

T

Tentacle Junkies
Humans who genetically modify themselves with grafted tentacles and more extreme forms. Live mostly in water. They are surprisingly numerous, and can be found on most of the settled worlds.

Tereshkova Port
The oldest and grandest of the Venusian cloud-cities. Tereshkova Port floats serenely above the poisoned atmosphere of Venus at one standard Earth gravity, synthesising water from the acid rain and offering spectacular views considered some of the best in the INNER SYSTEM. "See Venus and Die," as the old travel posters always said, and it remains a popular honeymoon destination.

Tong Yun City (Terminal)
The main city on Mars, and the main cultural and commercial

hub of the solar system. Home to the VATICAN OF THE ROBOTS, and the setting of many CHAINS OF ASSEMBLY episodes. It began life as Terminal, an ironic name given to it by the first settlers on a one-way trip in cheap jalopies.

Trifala King War
An ongoing, low-engagement conflict in and around the GALILEAN REPUBLICS.

U

Up and Out
Colloquial term mostly used on Earth to refer to the human worlds beyond the atmosphere.

Urbonas Ride
A form of euthanasia rollercoaster designed to provide a final thrill before death.

UXOs
Unexploded Ordnances. Generic term for old war machines, long since abandoned, which may yet explode or execute their prerogatives with lethal force if encountered.

V

Vatican of the Robots

Located on Level Three of Tong Yun City on Mars, at the heart of the city's Multifaith Bazaar deep underground (home to numerous churches, mosques, synagogues, Elronite and Gorean temples and the ubiquitous shrine to Ogko), little is known of the Robot Vatican. The few surviving robots are old and battered. Those who follow the Way of Robot designate themselves with an R. prefix. They choose among themselves one robot Pope, though some say it is not a robot at all but some sort of strange, giant computing machine. Followers of the Way of Robot see it as a holy duty to undertake, at one point in their rather long lives, a hajj or pilgrimage to the Vatican of the Robots. What the robots' ultimate purpose—if purpose be needed at all—is unclear. Rumours speak of a Heaven the robots are building in the zero-point field but, whether that has any truth in it or is merely a fanciful notion, nobody knows for sure.

W

Weather Hackers

Artists of dubious merit who hack local climate conditions (rain seeder drones, solar mirrors, wind generators and the like) in order to control weather.

Websters
People who, for one reason or another, now live as hermits, mostly through dislike or phobia of cities and/or other people.

Wildtech
Evolved, *verboten* technology, with such capabilities as human-hacking or military-grade destructive potential, virii and trojans and malware of all sorts, and all or none of the above. Wildtech uses NAKAIMAS technology, forbidden elsewhere in the solar system but widely available on JETTISONED, from where it inevitably departs to the rest of the solar system. Do not approach. Do not engage. But if exposed, it is probably already too late.

Wu Expedition
Mythical expedition of experienced explorers who went missing in the GUILDS OF ASHKELON universe while searching for the mythical PACMANDU.

X

Xanadu
Secretive compound of the Banu Qattmir (an outshoot of CLAN AYODHYA) in the Xanadu region of Titan. It holds most of the Titanic Cores. The three tenets of the Banu Qattmir are:

Security through Physicality.

Security through Redundancy.
Security through Obscurity.

Y

Year of Dragon
See DRAGON'S HOME

Yith
Humans with corrupted or hostile-intrusion-ridden NODES, turning them into shambling living corpses. It is suggested the YITH are a (perhaps accidental) by-product of the QUIETUDE.

Yiwu
Town in Eastern China, which manufactures the cheap everyday goods that most of the Earth needs—and indeed buys there. Yiwu is otherwise best known for its mysterious Lottery, in which the winner is guaranteed "their true heart's desire"—sometimes with unexpected results. Little is known of the Lottery, though its secretive organisation is believed to be present across the inhabited worlds.

Z

Zion, missing asteroid of
Asteroid in the Belt whose occupants used a novel form of

distributed small-world network utilising smoke particles as data carriers. It is believed the network was susceptible to outside interference, of what was once suggested to be a possibly alien source but may now be considered an outreach by the QUIETUDE. The Zion asteroid, utilising exo-fitted motors, subsequently went missing on an unknown trajectory.

Zoroaster
Ancient prophet and spiritual leader. Founder of Zoroastrianism.

EXCERPT FROM
CENTRAL STATION

I CAME FIRST TO CENTRAL STATION on a day in winter. African refugees sat on the green, expressionless. They were waiting, but for what, I didn't know. Outside a butchery, two Filipino children played at being airplanes: arms spread wide they zoomed and circled, firing from imaginary under-wing machine guns. Behind the butcher's counter, a Filipino man was hitting a ribcage with his cleaver, separating meat and bones into individual chops. A little farther from it stood the Rosh Ha'ir shawarma stand, twice blown up by suicide bombers in the past but open for business as usual. The smell of lamb fat and cumin wafted across the noisy street and made me hungry.

Traffic lights blinked green, yellow, and red. Across the road a furniture store sprawled out onto the pavement in a profusion of garish sofas and chairs. A small gaggle of junkies sat on the burnt foundations of what had been the old bus station, chatting. I wore dark shades. The sun was high in the sky and though it was cold it was a Mediterranean winter, bright and at that moment dry.

I walked down the Neve Sha'anan pedestrian street. I found shelter in a small shebeen, a few wooden tables and chairs, a small counter serving Maccabee Beer and little else. A Nigerian man behind the counter regarded me without expression. I asked for a beer. I sat down and brought out my notebook and a pen and stared at the page.

Central Station, Tel Aviv. The present. Or a present. Another attack on Gaza, elections coming up, down south in the Arava desert they were building a massive separation wall to stop the refugees from coming in. The refugees were in Tel Aviv now, centred around the old bus station neighbourhood in the south of the city, some quarter million of them and the economic migrants here on sufferance, the Thai and Filipinos and Chinese. I sipped my beer. It was bad. I stared at the page. Rain fell.

I began to write:

Once, the world was young. The Exodus ships had only begun to leave the solar system then; the world of Heven had not been discovered; Dr. Novum had not yet come back from the stars. People still lived as they had always lived: in sun and rain, in and out of love, under a blue sky and in the Conversation, which is all about us, always.

This was in old Central Station, that vast space port which rises over the twin cityscapes of Arab Jaffa, Jewish Tel Aviv. It happened amidst the arches and the cobblestones, a stone-throw from the sea: you could still smell the salt and the tar in the air, and watch, at sunrise, the swoop and turn of solar kites and their winged surfers in the air.

This was a time of curious births, yes: you will read about that. You were no doubt wondering about the children of Central Station. Wondering, too, how a strigoi was allowed to come to Earth. This is the womb from which humanity crawled, tooth by bloody nail, towards the stars.

But it is an ancestral home, too, to the Others, those children of the digitality. In a way, this is as much their story.

There is death in here as well, of course: there always is. The Oracle is here, and Ibrahim, the alte-zachen man, and many others whose names may be familiar to you—

But you know all this already. You must have seen The Rise of Others. *It's all in there, though they made everyone look so handsome.*

This all happened long ago, but we still remember; and we whisper to each other the old tales across the aeons, here in our sojourn among the stars.

It begins with a little boy, waiting for an absent father.

One day, the old stories say, a man fell down to Earth from the stars. . . .

Internationally renowned author Lavie Tidhar has been compared to Philip K. Dick by the *Guardian* and to Kurt Vonnegut by *Locus*. He works across genres, combining detective and thriller modes with poetry, science fiction, historical, and autobiographical material.

Tidhar's breakout novel *Central Station* received the John W. Campbell Memorial Award and the Neukom Literary Arts Award; it was nominated for the Arthur C. Clarke and Locus awards. *Central Station* has been translated into more than ten languages and won a Nebula Award in China.

Tidhar's next novel, *Unholy Land*, was a Prix Planète SF winner, shortlisted for the Locus, Campbell, Sidewise, and Dragon awards, and was on best of the year lists from *NPR Books*, *Library Journal*, and *Publishers Weekly*. Tidhar's 2021 novel, *The Escapement*, received the Special Citation for the

2021 Philip K. Dick Award and was a *Publishers Weekly* Top-10 Forthcoming Fantasy Title, a *Foreword* Book of the Day, and on the Locus Recommended Reading list. His other awards include the World Fantasy and British Fantasy Awards for his novel *Osama*, a British Science Fiction Award for Best Nonfiction, and the Jerwood Fiction Uncovered Prize for *A Man Lies Dreaming*.

In addition to his fiction and nonfiction, Tidhar is the editor of the acclaimed Apex Best of World Science Fiction series and a columnist for the *Washington Post*. His media appearances include Channel 4 News and BBC London Radio. His speaking appearances include Cambridge University, English PEN, and the Singapore Writers Festival. Tidhar has been a Guest of Honour at book conventions in Japan, Poland, Spain, Germany, Sweden, Denmark, China, and elsewhere. He is currently a visiting professor and Writer in Residence at Richmond, the American International University.

Lavie Tidhar grew up on a kibbutz in Israel and has lived all over the world, including South Africa, Vanuatu, Laos, and the UK. He currently resides with his family in London.

"It is just this side of a masterpiece.... Tidhar scatters brilliant ideas like pennies on the sidewalk."
—*NPR Books*

"Beautiful, original, a shimmering tapestry of connections and images."
—Alastair Reynolds

A worldwide diaspora has left a quarter of a million people at the foot of a space station. Cultures collide in real life and virtual reality. Life is cheap, and data is cheaper. But at Central Station, humans and machines continue to adapt, thrive, and even evolve.

"A wonder and a revelation—a work of science fiction capable of enthralling audiences across the multiverse."
—*Foreword*, starred review

Selected as an NPR, *Library Journal*, *Guardian*, and *Publishers Weekly* Best Book of 2018.

Lior Tirosh is a semi-successful author of pulp fiction, an inadvertent time traveler, and an ongoing source of disappointment to his father. World Fantasy Award winner Lavie Tidhar delivers a brilliantly subversive new novel that recalls *The Yiddish Policemen's Union* and *The City and the City*.

www.tachyonpublications.com

"Comic, tragic, and utterly magnificent—a masterpiece of fantasy . . . I can't wait to read it again."
—Samantha Shannon, author of *The Priory of the Orange Tree*

Into the Escapement rides the Stranger, a lone gunman on a quest to rescue his son in a strange parallel reality. In this dazzling new novel evoking Westerns, surrealism, epic fantasy, mythology, and circus extravaganzas, Lavie Tidhar has created an evocative dreamscape. *The Escapement* offers the archetypal darkness of Stephen King's *The Gunslinger* within the dark whimsy of a child's imagination.

"Like *Watchmen* on crack."
—*io9*

"If you love Philip K. Dick, Lavie Tidhar should be your new favorite writer"
—*The Jewish Standard*

A bold experiment has mutated a small fraction of humanity. Nations race to harness the gifted, putting them to dark ends. At the dawn of global war, flashy American superheroes square off against sinister Germans and dissolute Russians. Meanwhile, increasingly depraved scientists conduct despicable research in the name of victory.

www.tachyonpublications.com